SOCIETY WEDDINGS

*They're gorgeous, they're glamorous...
and they're getting married!*

Be our VIP guest at two of the most
talked about weddings of the decade—
lavish ceremonies where the cream of society
gather to celebrate these marriages
in dazzling international settings.

Welcome to the sensuous, scandalous world
of the rich, royal and renowned.

W9-BHX-523

SHARON KENDRICK started storytelling at the age of eleven and has never really stopped. She likes to write fast-paced, feel-good romances with heroes who are so sexy they'll make your toes curl! Born in west London, England, she now lives in the beautiful city of Winchester—where she can see the cathedral from her window (but only if she stands on tiptoe). She is married to a medical professor—which might explain why her family gets more colds than anyone else on the street—and they have two children, Celia and Patrick. Her passions include music, books, cooking and eating—and drifting off into wonderful daydreams while she works out new plots!

KATE WALKER was born in Nottinghamshire, England, but as she grew up in Yorkshire she has always felt that her roots are there. She met her husband at university and originally worked as a children's librarian, but after the birth of her son she returned to her old childhood love of writing. When she's not working she divides her time between her family, their three cats and her interests of embroidery, antiques, film and theater, and, of course, reading.

Sharon Kendrick
Kate Walker

SOCIETY WEDDINGS

HARLEQUIN®

TORONTO • NEW YORK • LONDON
AMSTERDAM • PARIS • SYDNEY • HAMBURG
STOCKHOLM • ATHENS • TOKYO • MILAN • MADRID
PRAGUE • WARSAW • BUDAPEST • AUCKLAND

ISBN 0-373-12268-3

SOCIETY WEDDINGS

First North American Publication 2002.

Copyright © 2002 by Sharon Kendrick and Kate Walker.

This edition published by arrangement with Harlequin Books S.A.

Visit us at www.eHarlequin.com

Printed in U.S.A.

Sharon Kendrick

PROMISED TO THE SHEIKH

CHAPTER ONE

THE man silhouetted against the shuttered window was not known as the Lion of the Desert for nothing. His skin glowed with tawny good health and his black hair was as thick as an ebony mane. The magnificence of his honed, muscular body had left countless women sighing with wistful longing and he carried about him an air of leonine grace and stealth.

Sheikh Rashid of Quador was a man few would have the folly to cross, and consequently his mood was usually as lazily unperturbed as a lion who was master and king of all he surveyed.

But for now his eyes glittered with icy displeasure.

'Repeat yourself, Abdullah,' he commanded, his deep voice as tightly controlled as a coiled whip.

His manservant swallowed nervously. 'Forgive me, Excellence—'

'Repeat yourself!' rang out the cold instruction.

Abdullah cleared his throat. 'There are...er...rumours sweeping the city, Sheikh.'

A pair of jet eyebrows were raised in silent yet imperious question. 'You dare to speak to me of rumours?'

'When they concern you, Excellency, then, yes—it is necessary that I should do so.'

'And?' he clipped out.

'Your people are growing restless, Sheikh.'

The black eyebrows were knitted together and fierce possessiveness gleamed like steel from the narrowed eyes. 'There is more rebellion underfoot? Insurrection that I must quash?'

'No, no—nothing like that, Sheikh. Your people accept that you rule them with an iron fist. The people of Quador live happily. They have food in their bellies and the security of

7

knowing that our profile in the modern world is a shining one—'

'Enough of compliments!' snapped Rashid. 'I have no need of them!'

'Indeed.' Abdullah sighed, the expression on his face not unlike that of a person who was anticipating a particularly painful visit to the dentist. 'The people of Quador wish to know why you have not yet taken a…wife,' he finished, with a weak smile.

'A *wife*?' The set of Rashid's lean body became dangerously tense and the hard, proud profile became stony. 'My people have no right to concern themselves in such matters! I shall take my bride when the time is right—and I alone will decide when that time is!' He thought fleetingly of Jenna and the black eyes gleamed anew, his voice transforming itself into a deceptively silky snare. 'But there is something else you are not telling me, is there not, Abdullah?'

'Indeed.' Abdullah swallowed. 'Reports from foreign newspapers have begun to infiltrate the internet—'

'The *internet*!' spat out Rashid. 'This internet is nothing but the work of the devil! It should be forbidden!'

'Yes, Exalted One,' agreed Abdullah placatingly. 'But if we are a member of the modern world, then it is impossible to halt progress!'

'And what *exactly* has infiltrated the internet?' demanded Rashid, his lush mouth flattening into a line of undisguised anger.

'Your…er…your relationship with a certain woman in Paris is causing some disquiet.'

'With Chantal?' Rashid felt the instinctive heavy pull of desire as he allowed his mind to linger briefly on the physical attributes of his most long-standing mistress. 'My friendship with Chantal is nothing new.'

'Precisely!' agreed Abdullah triumphantly. 'And its very endurance has provoked concern that you are perhaps planning to make *her* your wife!'

Rashid swore in French—one of the seven languages he was

fluent in. 'Are my people mad?' he questioned incredulously. 'You know which woman is promised to me!'

'Indeed,' murmured Abdullah.

'Do they not know that a man has many needs?' continued Rashid. 'What Chantal brings to me has nothing to do with marriage!' His mouth curved. 'It is not my destiny to marry a woman ten years my senior who will be unable to provide me with the many offspring I will one day desire!'

'That is as I thought, Exalted One.' Abdullah breathed a barely perceptible sigh of relief. He hesitated. 'Would you not make that message clear to the world? Has the time for offspring not now arrived?'

Rashid gave a heavy sigh and turned his face towards the window once more. Through the shutters, shafts of sunlight from the bright heat of the midday sun filtered through and illuminated his dark and golden beauty. In his tense, angry silence he was unmoving, as still as some hawk-nosed statue of a predatory conqueror.

Was the time now come? Was he indeed—ready?

He was known and feared for his resolute nature, for his steely intelligence and his decisiveness. It took him no more than a second or two to consider what had been plotted out for him since childhood, and then he nodded his dark head in answer to the silent question he asked himself.

Abdullah was his most trusted advisor, and the rumours must be gathering apace if he had summoned up the courage to alert his ruler to their existence.

And a man about whom uncertainty prevailed surely ran the risk of weakening his indomitable position…

He turned and surveyed the emotionless face of his envoy. 'So be it,' he said slowly. 'Destiny must at last prevail.' His eyes glittered with a cool acceptance and only the most lingering flash of regret, which was quickly replaced by the heat of sensual expectation. 'I will send for Jenna,' he stated softly. 'And the wedding will take place as soon as it can be arranged.'

*　　*　　*

Inside the wild and wonderful interior of her New York apartment the telephone began to shrill, and Jenna jumped.

'Can you answer that for me, Brad?' she called.

'Got it!'

Still damp from the shower, Jenna walked into the sitting room, a towel wrapped around her slim, glistening body and another draped in an elaborate turban around her head, just as Brad picked the receiver up.

The moment she saw the look on his face tiny little shivers of apprehension began to prickle at her skin. It was him; she knew it. She wasn't sure how, but she did.

Him.

Tiny beads of sweat broke out on her forehead, until she reminded herself that life had changed. That promises once made could be broken. The bond which had once existed between them had been silently yet inextricably severed. Surely it was inconceivable that he should demand what she had once most desired and now most feared.

'Jenna?' Brad was drawling in his soft American accent. 'Yeah, sure! She's right here. Hold on. I'll get her for you.' And he pulled a face as he handed her the phone.

Still trembling, Jenna took the receiver from him silently. 'Hello?'

There was a pause. 'Jenna?'

It *was* him. She would have known that voice anywhere, but then maybe that was because no other man in the world spoke like him. Steely-soft and velvet-hard. Sexy, predatory and distinctly unsettling. She swallowed, the modern woman she had become sorely tempted to say, Who's that? But she thought better of it. To affect not to know him would be to cast a slur on his character as well as denting his ego—and everyone knew that Sheikh Rashid of Quador had an ego the size of the United States itself!

'Rashid,' she said cautiously. She heard his terse exclamation in response, and knew that she had somehow angered him. 'How are you?' she asked in English.

'Who answered the phone?' he shot back—rather unexpectedly in the same language.

She considered telling him that it was none of his business, but again thought better of it. Rashid assumed that everything was his business, and that he had an inalienable right to have absolutely everything he wanted. But then he had been denied nothing from the moment of his birth—so maybe that was not so surprising.

'He's a friend of mine,' she informed him lightly. 'Brad.'

There was a moment of silence, and when he began to speak again there was not a trace of velvet—the voice was pure steel. And anger. *'Brad?'* he repeated on an incredulous note. 'A *man*? You have a *man* in your apartment?'

The irony wasn't lost on her: one rule for Rashid and another entirely different one for her. But much better to take the heat out of the situation with humour—for hadn't she once been able to make him laugh, a lifetime ago, before all her foolish girlhood dreams had been crushed underfoot, vanquished by the knowledge of just what kind of man he was? And what he did.

'I think so!' she joked rather nervously. 'Unless he's a master of disguise!'

In his stately study in the Quador palace, Rashid felt the slow burn of anger sizzle into rampant life. 'And how long has this *Brad*—' he spat the word out as if it was poison '—been your *friend*?'

Jenna clenched her fist around the receiver, so that her knuckles grew pale, but the instinctive movement brought with it a return of her resolve. Enough was enough! She was no longer his subject—not really. Hadn't her years in America and her new life here freed her from his influence?

But Rashid had the cunning of a fox—simple rebellion would not work with him. She did not yet know what he wanted, and until she did it was better to play the game. To slip into the role he would expect of her.

'Oh, ages,' she said vaguely, and then injected a note of docile interest into her voice. 'Did you just ring up for a chat, Rashid? Or was there something in particular you wanted?'

The 'something in particular' he wanted right now would have been to burst into her apartment and tear this Brad from limb to limb, demanding to know just who he was and what he had been doing... But Rashid drew himself back from expressing an emotion as wasted as jealousy, and instead allowed himself an arrogant smile. The one thing he *could* count on was that Jenna was as pure as the snows which topped the Quador mountains. Jenna...

His.

His.

Only ever *his.*

'I am displeased,' he said, with a silky and dangerous menace. 'Would you care to explain what he is doing there? Or do you make a habit of entertaining young men in your apartment?'

No, she would not care to explain herself, but she knew him well enough to realise that prevarication would be pointless. If any other man had spoken to her in that tone of voice she would have slammed the phone down. But this was a man like no other.

She thought about the dreams she had once cherished. Dreams about him which had taken on the quality of nightmares when she had learned the truth about him. At least living in America had allowed her to pretend that she was a different person from that foolish dreamer—and after a while it had became second nature to her and the pretence had become real. She *was* a different person.

And she would not let him spoil it now!

'What do you want, Rashid?' she sighed.

'I think that perhaps it was a mistake to allow you to study in America,' he observed in a hard voice.

'I disagree.'

'You *dare* to disagree with your sheikh?' he questioned mockingly, but Jenna realised that there was a hard ring of truth to his imperious question.

I dare to defy you! she wanted to shout, but if she did that then it would be all-out war—and there would only be one winner. She forced herself to put the sound of pleasure into her voice. Once it would have been genuine—there would have been delight there, too—but no more. 'At the time you put up few objections,' she pointed out.

'Because you twisted your father around your little finger!' he retorted. 'Convinced him that you should be allowed to travel. How persuasive you were, Jenna.'

'What is done is done, and the past is past,' she murmured in true Quador fashion. 'Now, come on, Rashid—do tell me to what pleasure I owe this phone call. *Such* a surprise,' she finished truthfully.

Rashid frowned. A surprise indeed, and several things had still not yet been explained. 'And where is your sister?' he questioned. 'Does she approve of this friend of yours, with whom you are so intimate that he sees fit to answer your phone for you?'

'Oh, don't be so old-fashioned!'

'But I am old-fashioned,' he told her silkily. 'Extremely old-fashioned. And you still haven't answered my question. Does your sister approve of this friend of yours?'

'Nadia approves of Brad,' said Jenna woodenly, but her eyes widened with an expression of fear as she stared into Brad's frowning face. If only Rashid knew that her sister was in love with Brad—that they were virtually living in the flat as man and wife. How his old-fashioned sensibilities would be outraged! 'He's a nice man,' she finished, and hoped that the fear had not crept into her voice.

'*Was* a nice man,' Rashid corrected coldly.

Now the fear was out in the open and she made no attempt to hide it. 'What do you mean by that?' she whispered hoarsely.

He gave a short, almost cruel laugh. 'Oh, I mean nothing more sinister than stating a fact, my sweet Jenna—simply that Brad and your life in New York will now become things of the past.'

'I think it's *your* turn to explain yourself,' said Jenna steadily, even though her heart was bashing madly against her ribcage.

'Can't you guess?' His voice had deepened into a beguiling caress. He remembered with a sudden deep ache the silken golden-brown of her hair and her deep amber eyes—so at variance with the other women of Quador. But she owed more than her looks to the inheritance of her American mother, he realised, a pulse beginning to beat at his temple. He wondered just how independent her life in New York actually *was*. And he wondered how many men 'friends' she had over there.

He should have put a stop to it long ago!

'The time has come, Jenna,' he said softly, and a sense of the inevitable began to heat his blood. He had embraced his destiny with a passion for all his life, and this particular destiny was no hardship.

Now she didn't care—she *would* affect to misunderstand him. Surely he could not mean what she suspected he was about to say next. 'Time for what?'

Rashid's mouth tightened. There had been little contact between them over the past four years, other than the formal and highly chaperoned meetings when she'd flown home to see her family, but that had been necessary for all concerned. Sensibilities had had to be preserved. And when he had gazed on the gleaming gold of her hair, and the lush, almost sinful curves of her body which even the traditional flowing Quador clothes could not disguise, he had been almost glad of the company of the chaperon. Had understood completely the need for their presence.

She had sent him dutiful letters from New York in which she portrayed a life which sounded almost dull due to overwork. And because of this he had been prepared to tolerate her short burst of freedom. As his wife she would be expected to dedicate her life to charitable works; this was surely not a bad way to begin?

And she was a highly intelligent woman... Far better to allow her a little leeway than to clip her wings completely.

He narrowed his eyes. 'I think you know very well what for, Jenna,' he snapped. 'It is time for you to return to Quador and become my wife!'

The hand that held the phone trembled. 'That's hardly the most romantic proposal I've heard!' But her laughter bordered on the hysterical and she saw Brad, who was still listening in to the conversation, stiffen with disbelief and alarm.

'If romance is what you seek from me, then better you should take the first plane home,' he instructed silkily, and he felt the blood heat in his veins, for opposition was rare enough to excite him!

Romance? She doubted whether he would understand romance if it came up and kicked him in the teeth! Gritting her own teeth together, she forced herself to stay calm with a huge effort of will.

'Rashid, you cannot still wish me to become your wife.' A note of desperation had now crept into her voice.

The heat died as her opposition began to irritate him. A little offered resistance was a game he could play as well as the next man, but enough was enough! She should be breathing soft sighs of gratitude down the phone at him by now! Planning her trousseau in her head!

'My *wishes* are not paramount,' he emphasised coldly. 'The agreement was made many moons ago, as well you know. But I will satisfy your every need as my wife, Jenna—of that you need have no doubts.'

She heard the raw, sexual boast which had deepened his voice and she shivered for all kinds of reasons—most of which she dared not even begin to analyse. Oh, yes, she knew exactly what he meant—and she *didn't* have any doubts. His prowess in the bedroom was legendary.

But Jenna had learnt much during her time in America—not least that women expected equality in a relationship. And equality with Rashid would be nothing but a distant dream.

Women expected something more, too—and that something was called love. Hopeless. For not only did she doubt Rashid's ability to give and receive love, she knew deep down that he would see such behaviour as a sign of weakness. Love made you vulnerable, and Rashid was the personification of invulnerability.

'Rashid,' she said, more weakly than she would have wished. 'You cannot mean that.'

There was an icy silence. Then, 'You may have the mistaken idea that sustained resistance is provocative, but let me tell you, Jenna, that you are wrong. You will be mine and you will return to Quador immediately. Is that understood?'

She forced herself to accept the inevitable, knowing that it was pure folly to deny him at least the second part of his command. She would return to Quador and she would be forced to play a cunning game herself. Soon Rashid would no longer want to marry her, but he must appear to have taken the decision himself. She must just make sure that he did.

The steely voice was speaking again. 'Still you hesitate,' he observed dangerously. 'Perhaps you wish for me to send someone to collect you?'

She blanched. Imagine one of Rashid's aides coming here and discovering the cosy domestic relationship between Nadia and Brad!

'No!' she protested. 'I'll book myself on the first available flight.'

'I will make sure that the first flight *is* available,' he said smoothly. 'A car will be awaiting you when you touch down in Quador, to bring you to the palace.'

And the connection was ended with a click.

CHAPTER TWO

JENNA put the receiver down with a hand which continued to tremble and looked up to see that Brad was standing there, the narrowed look of question still in his eyes.

'Jenna, what the hell is wrong?'

She stared at him. 'You do realise who that was?'

Brad nodded. 'Oh, yes,' he said grimly. 'I've heard enough stories from Nadia about his arrogant authority. I would have to be pretty dumb not to have guessed that it was Rashid. What the hell did he say to you? You look *awful*.'

It occurred to her that she was still standing wrapped in nothing but a towel, and a frisson of fear cooled her skin like ice-water being splashed on it.

What if Rashid sent one of his New York contacts to the apartment to make sure that she was obeying his command and preparing to leave? Someone could ring on the doorbell any second now, and wouldn't the situation look frighteningly compromising? She shuddered as she imagined his reaction to a report that she was cavorting half-naked in front of another man.

'Let me go and get dressed,' she said urgently, 'and then I'll tell you everything.'

In her bedroom she quickly pulled on a pair of jeans and a crisp white shirt, and combed through her long, damp hair before studying her reflection in the mirror.

She needed to act, and to act quickly! Rashid would never marry a woman whom he did not find attractive, and she would have to do everything in her power to make sure that he didn't. She would embrace the American side of her personality with a vengeance—and Rashid's immovable conservatism should do the rest!

Nodding resolutely at her pale face and widened amber

17

eyes, she returned to the sitting room, where Brad had made a pot of coffee. She took a mug from him gratefully, wrapping her long fingers around its steaming warmth and hoping that a little of it might creep its way into her heart.

She sat down on the sofa.

'So spill the beans,' he said quietly.

Jenna sighed, knowing that she did not have to ask Brad to keep what she was about to tell him completely confidential; he more than anyone knew how to keep secrets. 'He wants to marry me.'

Brad almost choked on his coffee. 'Say that *again*?' he demanded incredulously.

Jenna put the mug down and shook her head. 'Maybe I phrased that badly. I don't think he actually *wants* to marry me—it is just something he believes he must honour—an agreement which was made between our parents a long, long time ago.'

'Jenna—I don't have a clue what you're saying!'

She supposed that it must sound positively barbaric to a modern professional American man—and in truth didn't it sound more than a little barbaric to her? She sighed again, pushing a damp strand of hair from her cheek and fixing him with a candid look.

'I'll try to explain. Rashid's late father and my father were great, great friends—and when I was still in my cradle they decided that, provided I fulfilled certain...' She hesitated for a moment. 'Certain *criteria*, then I would one day make the perfect wife for Rashid.'

'And those criteria were what?' he questioned astutely.

Faint colour crept into her cheeks. 'Physically, I must be pleasing to Rashid's eyes—'

'Well, there couldn't be any doubt about that, surely?' he laughed.

False modesty would help no one. She shrugged. 'I understand that in that particular condition I met his specifications,' she answered slowly.

'You make it sound like the guy is picking out decor for a house!'

'Maybe it is a little like that,' she admitted, but she felt a shiver of memory as she recalled their last chaperoned meeting when she had surprised a hot, fleeting look of hunger in Rashid's enigmatic black eyes as he had greeted her. A look which had washed over her and made her skin tingle with awareness, even while the knowledge that Rashid desired her had filled her with fear and trepidation. 'The Ruler's needs must always be met. That is a given.'

'What other criteria?' asked Brad quietly.

Jenna bit her lip. 'The obvious one, of course. That I must go to him unsullied—but I really don't want to talk about that.'

Brad nodded. 'Sure,' he said understandingly. 'So what is it that you aren't telling me, Jenna? Surely the idea can't be that abhorrent to you? I've seen pictures of the guy and he sure looks like he fits the bill of conforming to most women's fantasy man!'

Jenna swallowed as unwilling images of his hard, lean body and cruel, dark face swam tantalisingly into her mind. 'Oh, no one is disputing Rashid's appeal,' she said carefully. 'Not even me. He is a most spectacular man. It's just that America has changed me—or rather knowledge has changed what I thought I once wanted.'

Brad pulled a face. 'You've lost me!' he protested.

Time had deadened some of the pain of discovery, but not all of it, and it still hurt to say it. 'When I first came to the States I had access to the free press for the first time in my life. I read newspapers with gossip columns—columns which documented Rashid's lifestyle with disturbing clarity.'

Brad nodded. 'I think I'm beginning to get the picture,' he said slowly.

Jenna splayed her hands over her thighs and curled her fingernails so that they bit into her through the denim. 'Rashid is almost twelve years older than I am,' she said. 'But when I was little he looked out for me—protected me.'

He had indulged her hero-worship of him. Taken her with him when he went falconing. And from the age of fourteen she had thought she would almost die with pleasure to see that formidable presence astride his night-dark stallion, subduing the bird of prey as if he could communicate with it by instinct alone. And maybe he could, she thought bitterly. For wasn't he a creature of prey himself?

Somewhere along the way she had acquired the rare ability to make him laugh, to gently tease him, and she had been the only person allowed to get away with what he would have regarded as insurrection in others. She had thought that the world began and ended with Rashid, and had grown to long for the wedding she knew must one day come.

'So what happened to make you hate him?' asked Brad.

Jenna lifted her head, surprised. 'Hate him? I'm not sure that I hate him.'

'You sound like you do—the way you talk about him.'

Did she? Wasn't hate too powerful an emotion to describe her feelings for Rashid? Too closely and dangerously linked to the flipside of such an emotion—love itself? A love which would never be anything more than one-sided and, consequently, never enough for the woman she had become.

Because when she had turned eighteen their relationship had changed fundamentally. Had it been the onset of womanhood which had made the magnificent sheikh grow so wary and distant in her company? she wondered. The atmosphere between them had been brittle with some kind of unnamed tension. Their earlier ease in each other's company had evaporated like the rare desert rains which sizzled beneath the intensity of the fierce Quador sun.

And she had missed that ease. Desperately. Without Rashid as her confidant she had felt as though she was in limbo— existing and not really living at all.

'Rashid made no move to marry me when I came of age,' she said slowly. 'And my pride wouldn't let me show my disappointment. I had no wish to stay in Quador, just waiting and waiting for some distant wedding, and so I told him that I wished to learn something of my late mother's country, that I wanted to study in America. It had always been her dearest wish that I should know something of her homeland.'

Rashid had had a great deal to cope with as well. His own parents had been killed in a plane crash, and his rightful inheritance had come much sooner than anyone had anticipated. As well as coping with his grief he had had to come to terms with governing a vast country. It had not been an easy transition as power was transferred to the handsome young Sheikh. Many had doubted he would be able to stamp his dominance onto the demanding land and Rashid had been determined to prove them wrong.

She remembered the thoughtful way he had considered her request to study law in America, consulting long and hard with her father before they had both given her their consent.

'I admit that I found his blessing to leave both upsetting and confusing, but the reason for this soon became crystal-clear.' She let out a painful, shuddering breath as she remembered the newspaper clippings. 'The truth hurt,' she told him quietly.

'What truth?' Brad questioned.

'The truth about his lifestyle. How very foolish I was,' she said with a bitter laugh. 'I thought that as I was promised to him he would forsake all others. How naive could you get? I soon discovered that Rashid had been involved with supermodels and actresses since he was a teenager. The news had been kept from me while I lived in Quador, but I found out soon enough once I moved away. Why, he even has a mistress at the moment—it is well documented enough. He shares another woman's bed in Paris even while he summons me back for our wedding!'

'Are you sure?' asked Brad, in a horrified voice.

'Perfectly sure. Her name is Chantal and she is his favourite. No doubt she will occupy a nearby hotel even during our honeymoon—such are the customs in Quador!'

He flinched. 'So what the hell are you going to do, Jenna? Surely you aren't going to allow yourself to tolerate a union like that?'

'Oh, no,' she said with quiet fervour, and allowed herself a small smile of determination. 'I shall go back to Quador and convince Rashid that I am not the woman he wishes to marry.'

'And how will you do that?'

The smile died on her lips. She must waste no more time,

and neither must she involve Nadia or Brad in her decisions—
for Rashid would not tolerate collusion. She shivered. The
consequences for her sister would be unimaginable. 'I'll think
of something,' she said airily, and smiled as she stood up.
'Don't worry about *me*, Brad,' she said.

'But I do,' he said, with a shrug.

She looked affectionately at the man her sister loved with
such a passion. 'Well, don't,' she remonstrated softly. 'I do
not intend to let him bully me into doing something to which
I am morally opposed.'

He didn't look convinced. 'Sure,' he said. And neither did
he sound it.

Jenna tossed the golden-brown hair off her shoulders like a
feisty young mare preparing for flight. 'And now I'm going
to book my flight and pay a visit to the stores.'

Rashid's plane touched down in Paris and a darkened limou-
sine was waiting to whisk him away to the luxurious apartment
situated in the sixth *arrondissement*, the city's most prestigious
area.

As always, one discreet bodyguard preceded him while another hovered unseen to the rear. When they reached the door
Rashid nodded his head and held his hand out for the leather
case the other man carried.

'You may leave me now,' he instructed.

'But Exalted One—'

'Leave me!' Rashid rasped. 'I will make my presence
known to you shortly.'

The bodyguard narrowed him a look which said that he
objected to the Sheikh's insistence, but he knew that such ob-
jection was pointless.

'Yes, Excellency.'

Rashid rang the bell. He had his own key, but he knew that
he could no longer use it.

The door opened and Chantal stood before him. She had
been expecting him—his phone call earlier that day had been
rapturously received, as was normal. Just for a moment his
mouth tightened as he thought how *Chantal* would have re-

sponded to his proposal of marriage. With pleasure, and joy, and with hunger. And the contrast between the almost insulting uninterest which Jenna had displayed filled him once more with the slow burn of anger.

'*Chéri*, your unexpected visit has brought me much pleasure,' murmured Chantal, and like a vixen she moved towards him, all perfume and silk and shockingly provocative experience as she held her arms out.

But he took a step back and shook his head, and although she shrugged with disappointment she still followed him unquestioningly into the huge sitting room with its spectacular views over Paris.

He watched her for one last time. As a mistress she had been matchless. Utterly matchless. Her looks belied her forty-four years and her body was sleeker and more toned than that of a woman half her age. The raven hair gleamed and moved with the careless abandon which only the finest hairdresser could construct, and the deceptively simple green silk dress must have cost a king's ransom. And what Chantal didn't know about the art of lovemaking simply wasn't worth knowing.

His mouth tightened again.

'A drink, *chéri*?' she murmured, and her voice dropped into husky entreaty. 'Or shall I run you a bath?'

In the past he might have had both. Or neither. He might rip the expensive dress from her body and it would simply excite her, make her part her pale thighs eagerly for him.

But no more.

He shook his head. 'My car is waiting.'

'So?'

'Chantal, there is something that I must tell you—'

She stilled, her eyes narrowing with suspicion as something in the tone of his voice must have warned her, and he realised that she was woman of the world enough to know that the news he had come to bring to her today would not be to her liking.

Defiantly, she reached for her cigarettes and lit one. 'Then tell me, *chéri*—do not keep me in suspense!'

'I'm getting married.'

She didn't react, just blew the smoke out in one long, deep breath, the perfect arch of her eyebrows elevating only very slightly.

'So I must offer my congratulations, must I?' she questioned coolly.

He smiled. From the almost supercilious mask she wore it was impossible to guess at her true feelings. But then, she had never shown him her true feelings—and hadn't that been one of qualities he had most admired about her? 'Thank you.'

She drew deeply on the cigarette. 'Who is she?'

'Jenna.'

She nodded, and then the mask slipped and a calculating look sharpened her beautiful features. 'The girl who is half-American? She lives in New York?'

Rashid frowned. Had he told her so much? 'The very same.'

'She must be overjoyed.'

Rashid's mouth tightened again. She *should* be overjoyed, though her attitude had been a million miles away from the gratitude he had been expecting. But Jenna would soon learn never to try to resist his wishes again!

'What woman wouldn't be?' asked Chantal sadly, before he could answer. She stubbed the cigarette out with a vicious movement of her fingers and began to unbutton her dress. 'So this will be the last time for us, *chéri*? Or will you still have time for me once you are *married*?'

He could see the pale thrust of her breasts contrasted against the lace of the exquisite lingerie she wore and he felt his body hardening with the slow, relentless pulse of desire. But he quashed it as ruthlessly he would a scorpion which could sometimes be found lurking beneath stones in the unforgiving desert.

'No,' he said roughly. 'Stop that!'

She moved her fingers beneath her dress, drifting her fingertips provocatively against herself, and her eyes widened alluringly as she began to move her hips with slow, sensual rhythm. 'Are you sure, *chéri*?' she whispered huskily.

A muscle worked in his cheek as he dropped the leather

case he was carrying onto the chair in front of her. 'Yes, I am certain!' His voice was harsh. 'Do your dress up! Now!'

She stared into his face for a long moment and began to do as he had ordered, the pallor of her cheeks the only outward sign of her distress.

'The apartment is yours to keep,' he said.

She nodded. 'Thank you,' she said heavily.

He had known that she would not refuse. 'And I have brought you something.' He indicated the box with a stabbing movement of his finger.

'What is it?'

He opened it up and row upon row of glittering diamond brooches lay there in dazzling array against a backdrop of dark velvet. He saw the look of natural indulgent pleasure as she surveyed them, before lifting her eyes to his in cool appraisal.

'For services rendered?' she enquired, with a wry smile.

He shook his head. 'As a small symbol of my gratitude for such an enjoyable relationship.'

The pleasure was replaced by alarm. 'It needn't be over, Rashid,' she said urgently. 'You know that.'

Yes, he knew that. She could be his for the taking, whenever and wherever he wanted. Jenna need never know, need never find out—he had countless people who would cover for him without question. It would be almost expected of him to behave as his father had done.

But he shook his head. 'It is over, Chantal,' he said roughly, and indicated the jewellery with a casual wave of his dark-skinned hand. 'Take your time. Choose the one which pleases you most, and I will arrange to have the remainder collected by Abdullah.'

She nodded and stared at him. 'So that's it?'

'You knew that this would happen some day. It was as inevitable as the dawn which follows night. So let us have no regrets, and let us remember the past with affection.' He glanced down at the costly timepiece which gleamed so palely gold against his dark wrist. 'It is time for me to leave. My plane is waiting.'

She nodded, and abruptly turned away from him. 'Goodbye,

chéri,' she whispered, but he heard the hint of tears in her voice.

'Goodbye, Chantal,' he said softly.

He was almost at the door when she halted him with a word. 'Wait!'

He turned around, but he didn't need to look into her face to know what was coming next.

'If ever—*ever*—you change your mind, you know that I'll be here for you, Rashid.'

He gave a hard smile. 'Goodbye, Chantal,' he repeated, and without another word he turned on his heel and left her apartment.

CHAPTER THREE

As SOON as Jenna emerged from the plane the blazing temperature of Quador hit her, and it was like being punched in the face by a blazing fist.

The flight had been mildly eventful merely for the fact that as soon as she had arrived at Kennedy Airport she had been upgraded to first class, and it didn't take a genius to guess who was behind that.

She had started to protest, but then her words had tailed away uselessly and she had seen the check-in girl looking at her with ill-disguised curiosity, as if wondering who in their right mind would object to flying home in unadulterated luxury on Quador Airlines.

Abdullah, Rashid's chief aide, was standing on the Tarmac waiting for her, next to the dark-windowed car which bore Rashid's distinctive crest, and he bowed his head respectfully as she approached. Though not before she had seen the small triumphant gleam in his eyes.

He knows! she thought. He knows the purpose of my visit! But Abdullah was very much of the old school of courtier, and she suspected that he thought Rashid was long overdue in taking a bride for himself.

'Did you have a pleasant flight?' he asked courteously, as the powerful car was waved straight through all the normal barriers without question.

'A wonderful, smooth flight,' replied Jenna truthfully. She certainly wasn't about to start enlightening Abdullah about the nervous churning in her stomach as she had contemplated what she was about to do.

Rashid's palace was situated in an isolated spot just outside the main city of Riocard itself, its solitary location necessary for grim and practical reasons. There had been several assassination attempts on Rashid's father, and on his predecessors too, and Jenna wondered whether Rashid had also been a target for the many fanatics who would wish to rule Quador themselves.

She turned her head to look out through the window, unprepared for the leap of distress in her heart which her thoughts caused. But she reasoned that just because she had no wish to marry the man that did not mean she would wish to see him hurt.

Rashid hurt! Jenna gave a wry smile. It seemed as unlikely and as incongruous an idea as trying to imagine Rashid being celibate!

The palace itself was centuries old, with formal terraces and magnificent pillars carved with figures of Rashid's ancestors. The grounds had been modelled on a larger scale of some beautiful English country-house garden, and the well-tended lawns were almost indecently green. A large and decorative rectangular pond glittered back the reflection of the blazing sun and Jenna found herself wishing that she could trail her fingertips through its soothing coolness.

The car slid smoothly through the vast, ornate gates which were guarded by lynx-eyed men who carried poorly concealed guns and Jenna shivered, looking around at the formal security with new eyes. If it seemed like a different world, then that was because it *was*, and she had grown accustomed to, grown to love, the freedom and ease of her life in America.

'The Sheikh is waiting for you in his private apartments,' said Abdullah. 'I suggest that we do not keep him waiting.'

Suggestion, indeed! It was nothing but a smoothly broached command, and Jenna nodded, feeling a little like the sacrificial lamb going to the slaughter.

She mounted the curving marble staircase with a growing feeling of dread, and even the sight of the exquisite mosaics in every hue of blue imaginable, the priceless chandeliers which hung in crystal waterfalls from the ceiling, could do little to quell her fears. She had always loved the palace, but today it looked like nothing more than a gilded prison.

The guard outside Rashid's apartments pushed open the heavy door.

'Your case will be brought from the car for you,' murmured Abdullah, and he raised his eyebrows. 'You have travelled lightly, I note.'

Well, of course she had—she wasn't planning on staying! 'Very lightly,' she agreed, with a tight smile.

'Very well. I will take my leave of you now, mistress,' said Abdullah, and he bowed his head.

'Thank you, Abdullah.'

Jenna stepped inside the room, praying for the serenity to see her plan through without giving herself away. But in spite of her misgivings her mouth dried instinctively as she saw Rashid silhouetted against the window. A high-born female chaperon was sitting demurely on one of the brocade window seats close by.

Had she ever thought that her refusal to marry him was going to be easy? A piece of cake? Had she simply forgotten his magnificence, and the effect it always had on her? she wondered distractedly. Or simply trained herself not to dwell on it, because then she could disregard the fact that he still had the power to fill her with a hopeless yearning?

Even now.

Dressed in traditional flowing robes of cloth-of-gold, his muscular body seemed more vital than that of any other man she had ever laid eyes on, and her traitorous heart reminded her of how much she had once adored him. And trusted him.

He heard her enter, but he did not turn. Not immediately. She had kept him waiting for two days since his telephone call summoning her here, and now he would make her wait before she could feast her eyes on the stern face of the man to whom she would soon be joined! He felt the first stirrings of desire, but he did not allow his mind or his body to linger on such thoughts. First he must dispense his disapproval!

Jenna knew what was expected of her. Reminding herself that to anger him would not help her case, she spoke one word in the demure voice she had practised in her head over and over again during the flight from New York.

'Sheikh.' It was both an acknowledgment and a deference, and there was a split-second pause before she saw him half incline his proud head. And then, very deliberately, he turned around to face her, and the dryness in her mouth increased, as did the acceleration of her heart.

How *could* she have forgotten his physical presence? For he was magnificent! Utterly, utterly magnificent! The carved face so cruelly perfect, the coal-black eyes gleaming with a fierce and icy intelligence. And something else, too.

Not anger, no. Anger would be too mild a word to describe the emotion which was sizzling its way across the room at her.

Fury.

Stark, undisguised fury.

She should have been expecting it, had told herself to expect it, but even Jenna was unprepared for her shivering response to the vision of the formidable Rashid slanting her a look of total condemnation.

'What have you been doing to yourself?' he hissed at her, like an angry serpent who had been disturbed. He spoke in French, presumably so that the chaperon would not understand, but the soft, sensual-sounding words only reminded Jenna of his mistress, and it was as though someone had driven a stake through her heart with all the force they could muster.

She lifted her eyes to his, feigning ignorance of his question. 'Sheikh?' she questioned, with a very credible line in demure confusion.

Again, Rashid felt the blood heating his veins, but this time not with desire—no, certainly not that! For the woman who stood before him bore such little resemblance to the Jenna he remembered that he scarcely recognised her.

She wore tight blue jeans and a silky amber top which matched her huge eyes and emphasised the luscious swell of her breasts. High-heeled snakeskin ankle-boots made even more of the length of her long, slim legs, where the denim clung to them so provocatively. So very Westernised, he thought, in disgust, as he let his cold and disapproving gaze travel to her head, where a wide-brimmed and flower-decked straw hat was managing to conceal all the silken splendour of her hair.

But it was the make-up which caused the little pulse to beat so forbiddingly at his temple. Quador women—and particularly high-born Quador women—did not mar their complexions with the false glitter of cosmetics!

He scowled.

There was a subtle golden glow which shimmered over the heavy lids of her deep-set eyes, and the long lashes were ebony-dark and spiked like the legs of a spider. Her full lips gleamed provocatively, highlighted with some rose-pale tint, and whilst the man in him could not deny that she looked very beautiful indeed, he also knew something else.

That she looked like a tramp!

More mistress than wife!

'How dare you come before me so attired?' he demanded imperiously.

'You don't like my clothes?' she questioned innocently.

He would like to tear them from her back! Fighting down the urge to storm across the room and do just that—for he could not ignore the watchful eye of the chaperon—he steadied himself with a deep breath.

'You look like a tramp!' he offered, giving voice to his thoughts.

'Hardly,' answered Jenna drily. 'A tramp would ill be able to afford the cost of *this* outfit!'

'Not *that* kind of tramp!' he contradicted icily. 'The kind of tramp to be found hanging around the back streets of Riocard!'

'Oh, you mean a prostitute?' she questioned helpfully.

Furiously, he ignored that. 'Why did you not come to me wearing traditional Quador dress?'

'Because this is the kind of thing I'm more used to! It's all the rage in New York!'

'Why?' he snarled. 'Does *Brad* like you to dress like that?'

Jenna realised that she was straying into dangerous and uncharted waters. And that she was supposed *not* to be antagonising him! 'I'll go and change,' she offered, but he shook his head.

'Oh, no, you won't,' he said grimly. 'You have kept me waiting too long. You will leave only when I give you leave to!' He drew another deep breath. 'Would you like some refreshment after your journey?' he forced himself to say.

She felt like asking him if he was offering tea or hemlock, but thought better of it. She shook her head, and the movement drew his eye and caused another small snarl of irritation.

'Remove your hat!' he ordered.

This was it. The moment which would confirm her conversion from Suitable Wife to Sassy American! With one easy movement she pulled the straw hat from her head, though her heart was pounding nervously as she stared at him with an expression she prayed was not *too* defiant.

For a moment Rashid was speechless. If she had suddenly started flying around the State Apartments he could not have been more profoundly shocked.

'But you have cut your hair!' he observed in a strangled kind of voice.

For one bizarre and crazy moment Jenna thought that he sounded almost *sad*, but nerves must have made her imagination work overtime. And when she met the steel of his eyes she knew that she must have been mistaken.

'Yes. Do you like it?' she asked lightly, and felt the air-conditioning cool her newly bare neck.

'*Why?*' he demanded hoarsely as he remembered the silken strands of syrup-coloured hair which had streamed down almost to her bottom. A pulse leapt in his groin. He had imagined untying it on their wedding night, had pictured it spread out across his chest, contrasting so beautifully against the dark skin. 'Why shave your head like that? To look like a man? No longer a woman?'

Something in his criticism made Jenna forget her vow not to anger him any more than was necessary. His look of pure censure offended some very elemental emotion deep inside her, and the look he was lancing her way made her fleetingly wish that she had not opted for such a dramatic cut, that she could win back his approval.

Until she reminded herself of Chantal, and of all the others. Let *them* crave his approval—she would make herself tolerate his contempt!

Or would she?

Was it feminine pride which made her draw her chin up and pull her shoulders back in haughty query? The movement caused her breasts to push imperceptibly against the silk shirt, and she saw from the sudden tensing of his body that it had not escaped Rashid's attention.

The chaperon, whose job it was to protect but not to intrude, was listening to the conversation but unable to understand it. She was not looking at them either, her hands busy with some prayer beads.

So she would have missed the look of raw, feral hunger which had darkened Rashid's eyes to pure ebony. And the dull flush of colour which crept over his arrogantly carved cheekbones.

If a look could be X-rated, then Rashid had just invented it! Refusing to be intimidated—or tempted—by the undisguised sexual hunger which emanated from his body, Jenna stared back at him, even though she was acutely aware of the stinging of her breasts and the heated rush of some honeyed feeling which was making her knees feel very weak indeed.

'You think I look like a man?' she challenged softly.

Had something in the air around them changed? For the chaperon lifted her head and frowned, but Rashid paid her no heed. She was his subject, and here only to ensure that neither the man nor the woman touched each other.

'Go back to your beads!' he commanded in his native tongue, and the woman obeyed him instantly.

He reverted to French, and gave a small nod of his dark head in the direction of the chaperon. 'You see? That is the kind of compliance I am used to, Jenna. The kind of compliance I expect,' he purred, mesmerised by the tight little buds which were pushing against her shirt.

She would be responsive, his Jenna, he thought, with a sudden heady rush of elation and power. Maybe he had always instinctively known that, but now he was certain. He would make her weep with pleasure in his arms. He would captivate and subdue her until she wanted him and only him, and he would tutor her desire until it matched his own!

'Not from me,' she said instantly. 'I am not your subordinate! I have lived too long in America not to consider a man and a woman to be equals!'

He stiffened with outrage. 'How do you dare to speak thus to your Ruler?' he demanded incredulously. 'When we are wed you will *naturally* take on the subordinate role of wife!'

His arrogant boast drew her up short. This wasn't going as well as she had hoped. In fact, that was the understatement of the year! He should be gradually going off the idea of marriage to her by now. Minute by minute, his resolve should be weakening. She decided to play the equality card a little bit more.

Defiantly, she raked her fingers through the starkly cropped hair. 'I'm pretty pleased with it myself,' she confided, and gave him a bright smile. 'So easy to manage. I can go straight to college with it still wet from the shower. Just like a man, actually!'

His eyes became cold chips of jet. *'Still wet from the shower?'* he repeated tightly. 'You go to college with your hair wet?'

She supposed that it must sound bizarre to a man whose position had always isolated him from the cares and concerns of normal everyday life—but he was making it sound as though she had committed some kind of sexual deviation. 'Of course!' she expanded. 'If I'm late.'

He expelled a low breath. 'Well, you will not have such concerns in the future, because you will not be studying from now on, Jenna! And you will grow your hair immediately!'

Jenna stared at him in alarm. This wasn't what she had intended to happen at all!

Deep in her heart she knew that her objections to him were well founded. It wasn't just the fact that he was an irrepressible seducer with great streams of women waiting to leap into his beds—his arrogance was even more breathtaking than she had remembered!

But then she had never openly opposed him before.

Imagine what kind of autocratic and overbearing husband he would make! Worse than in her very worst nightmares.

She had hoped that it wouldn't come to this, but she knew she had no choice. There was one thing and one thing only which would guarantee her a seat on the very next plane out of Quador.

Her voice was remarkably steady as she said, 'But I can't marry you, Rashid. It...it wouldn't be fair.'

The black eyes glittered with interest. 'Oh?'

She swallowed, and now her voice was not so steady. 'B-because I am no longer fit to be your wife,' she breathed. 'You see, I have already taken a lover before you, Rashid. I am no longer pure. And therefore I cannot marry you.'

CHAPTER FOUR

HELL broke loose.

Rashid harshly uttered a Quadorian curse, then added a few more in English and French and Spanish to really get the message home. Then he strode over to Jenna, his face a livid picture of dark fury, and the chaperon sprang to her feet in alarm.

'Excellency!'

'Silence!' he thundered autocratically, and the chaperon sat straight down again.

His rage was so potent that he felt consumed by it, as if it had invaded his very blood—but alongside that rage came the desire to beat his fist uselessly against the wall. Jenna! His Jenna—in bed with another man! He wanted to kill him!

'I want his name!'

And then to kill her!

'Well, you can't have it!' Jenna backed away from him, recoiling as much from the expression on his face as from his anger. And if she had thought that she had seen contempt there before, then she had been wrong. *This* was contempt—a contempt so blisteringly undiluted that it seemed to sizzle off him in hot and tangible waves.

She forced her stumbling words out with difficulty. 'R-Rashid, I realise that this means that you can't marry me—w-won't *want* to marry me—and I'm sorry if it's ruined all your plans. But I think the best thing is if I just get straight back on the plane to America and—'

'Silence!' he thundered, cutting across her babble with the gunfire shot of his voice. He controlled his breathing with difficulty. He could never remember feeling quite so outraged before. Nor so shocked. With a supreme effort of will he banished the disturbing vision of Jenna lying naked and entangled

with another from his mind. His black eyes narrowed, but the
gleam that spat from them was like a searchlight. 'Was it
Brad?' he questioned softly.

Her eyes widened. 'No!' she gasped.

He nodded. Her reaction had been too instant to be a lie.
Instinct told him that. 'Then who?' he pursued, with deadly
intent.

She shook her head, wishing that her long hair was back to
camouflage her flaming cheeks. 'Rashid, I must go,' she said
desperately.

'Not yet,' he contradicted implacably, and traced a thoughtful forefinger along the shadowed jut of his chin.

He did not speak for a moment, and when he did his words
startled her. 'It is inconceivable that you leave Quador without
first seeing your father,' he murmured. 'And you really need
to freshen up before you do so.' His eyes swept over her
disparagingly. 'Don't you?'

Was he really letting her off so lightly? Jenna let out an
inaudible sigh of relief. Maybe she had just unwittingly provided the answer to his unspoken wishes. She had let him off
the hook and he could continue his playboy activities to his
heart's content—without the prospect of a jealous wife watching his every move.

And he did have a point. She had come straight here after
a long flight, directly into the heat of the Quador day. She was
hot and she was sticky. Once she bathed and made herself
respectable she could visit her father.

She shuddered. Would Rashid tell him? She met the coldness of his eyes and her tongue snaked out in a vain attempt
to moisten her dry lips. She saw his eyes darken in angry
response. 'Yes,' she said quietly. 'I would like to bathe and
change, and then I will be gone from your life for ever.'

His smile was cruel. How naïve she was if she thought that
she could drop a bombshell like that and simply walk away
from the devastation she had caused! But he merely nodded
his head. 'Very well, Jenna,' he agreed equably. 'Your chaperon will show you to a private set of apartments, and you
will make use of them as you please.'

Swallowing nervously, she nodded. In truth, she had not expected his anger to subside so quickly. She had thought that his pride would be offended more than anything—and didn't it almost *hurt* that he now seemed to be accepting the situation with apparent calm? Maybe Rashid was more modern and more tolerant than she had imagined him to be.

But one sneaking look at the unyielding face told her not to push her luck, and to get out of there before he changed his mind.

He barked out an instruction and the chaperon nodded, beckoning Jenna to follow her.

Unseeingly, she left the State Rooms and walked in the footsteps of the older woman through a maze of palace corridors, her heart pounding painfully with relief and an aching sense of regret for what could now never be. It wasn't until she was safely inside a dim, cool bedchamber, where her one suitcase lay unopened on the bed, that her pulse began to die down to something approaching normality.

'You wish that I should stay and assist you?' asked the chaperon, but Jenna shook her head.

She needed solitude to get her jumbled thoughts and emotions in some kind of order. She needed to compose herself and present a calm façade to her father—and she certainly couldn't begin to do that if she had an audience. Particularly an audience with such curious eyes. She shook her head. 'Thank you, but, no. I am used to managing on my own.'

Once the woman had quietly closed the door behind her Jenna sank with trembling knees onto the low, wide divan on which most high-born Quadors slept, and buried her face in her hands.

If she lived to be a hundred she would never forget that look of haunted disillusion which had fired Rashid's face, so that for a moment he had resembled the devil himself. And she found herself remembering with poignant longing the expression of indulgent tenderness with which he'd used to look at her, so very long ago.

But it was too late for that now. She had sealed her fate with her words, and Rashid would never forgive her. She must just pray that he would be reasonable enough never to repeat what she had told him to her dear father.

She forced herself into action. The sooner she acted, the sooner she could be out of here. She filled the deep circular bath with water and oils scented with jasmine, and stripped off her jeans and her silky top. She threw them on the bed, together with her underwear.

Then she opened the suitcase and pulled from it a traditional Quador outfit, her breath escaping in a shuddering sigh as she laid it carefully on the bed.

The soft, silken robes brought back memories of happier times. In a way she had missed their filmy respectability—the long flowing tunic and the wide trousers worn beneath. A woman could feel like a real woman when concealed in the soft, sensual caress of silk.

She bit her lip as she lowered her body into the bath and closed her eyes.

She lay there for long, timeless moments, until lethargy began to seep into her limbs, and then she washed herself with the delicious scented soap and wrapped herself in a towel. She walked back into the bedchamber to find the room filled with an unexpected presence.

A dark, powerful and brooding figure awaited her, and her heart very nearly stopped.

'R-Rashid,' she stumbled foolishly. 'W-what on earth are you doing here?' But the look in his eyes told its own story, and her heart picked up its beat again as she shrank from the ebony blaze of his eyes.

He had come here to gather facts, or at least that was what he had convinced himself during his furious march through the palace. He had intended to do nothing more than tell her that the thought of her with another man had tainted his view of her for ever. But one sight of her curved and slender body, even the boyish haircut, had driven away reason and left him with nothing but the insistent clamouring of his senses. He was on fire with a need that consumed him.

'I'll leave why I'm here to your own imagination, Jenna,' he said, his voice menacingly soft.

To think that all the while he had been rejecting Chantal's sensual invitation Jenna had been cavorting with some unknown man on the other side of the world! The rage burned so bright within him that he felt he might explode with it.

'And I am sure it is a very vivid imagination these days, is it not? Has your American lover taught you much?' Dark eyebrows were arched in arrogant and erotic query. 'Perhaps your new-found knowledge is such that you would like to share it with me?'

She understood his meaning instantly. 'S-stop it!' she gasped, but she was speaking as much to her own body as to the sexual predator who stood so tense with expectation beside the divan.

What was happening to her?

Because, somehow, the way that he was looking at her with a mixture of desire and contempt was igniting forbidden dreams that she had thought long-vanished.

A cruel smile curved his delicious lips. 'Stop what?' he questioned, almost conversationally. 'I'm merely elaborating on what you have just told me—giving you the opportunity to demonstrate your *liberation*!' He spat the last word out as if it were poison.

'I think you'd better go, Rashid,' she said in a low voice. She dropped her gaze from his so that he wouldn't see the hot, answering hunger in her eyes, which was making her breasts tingle so intensely that it was a sensation close to exquisite pain. 'I'd like to get dressed now.'

The smile became even more cruel. 'But that would oppose the wishes of your Ruler, Jenna.'

She lifted her eyes in horrified and excited understanding. 'You can't mean—'

'Oh, but I can. I do not wish to see you dressed. On the contrary—your naked body is all I desire. I want you, Jenna—and I want you now. For too long I have played the assiduous gentleman around you. Fool! When all the time...'

He began to move towards her, and it was so close to all her illicit half-forgotten fantasies that she was frozen there, like a statue waiting to be brought to life by the man she had always desired more than any other.

He was nothing but a breath away now, all dark and golden stealth, muskily rapacious. 'If I had but known...' he continued, and reached his hand out to run his fingertips over the long, bare line of her neck, feeling it tremble in response. 'If I had but known that you were in need of a man's body, then I should have oh, so willingly complied with your wishes.'

'G-go away,' she said helplessly.

His voice deepened as he saw her body sway instinctively towards his. 'But you don't want me to. You want me, Jenna. You always did. And now you always will. You will ache with the memory of what you have thrown away for the rest of your days. That will be my curse on you!'

He pulled the towel away from her unprotesting fingers, and as it fell redundantly to the ground he sucked in a raw breath of longing as she stood naked before him, her body more beautiful than he had dreamt of, even in his wildest dreams.

Her skin gleamed as if of gold, with dark and secret shadows, and the lush swell of her breasts was tipped with dark rose. He sucked in a shuddering breath as he felt his body jerk into life.

'May the desert always bloom!' he groaned thickly, and pulled her urgently into his arms to kiss her, more excited than he had ever been in his life.

Melded tightly against him, Jenna could feel every lean, hard contour of his body through his silken robes, even while his mouth worked its predictable magic, and then she was lost from all sane thought. Many times she had imagined a kiss like this, and yet the reality blew the fantasy away in meaningless little pieces.

'R-Rashid,' she whispered shakily, lacing her fingers possessively in his hair, as she had wanted to do for as long as she had been a woman.

He groaned again as he reached down to cup one breast, feeling its ripe, warm weight nestling in the palm of his hand while his thumb teased the hardening nub with an expertise which had her almost fainting. 'Rashid, what?' he questioned unsteadily. 'Rashid, make love to me? Rashid, join me to your body? Is that what you want, Jenna?'

May God forgive her—because that was *exactly* what she wanted! She gave no answer, merely a fraught little whimper of assent, because now his hand was splayed possessively over the slight swell of her belly and was moving down between her thighs. She should have felt frightened, but all she felt was a deep, almost unbearable sensation of longing.

And then he found her, touched her where she was filled with heat, and she bucked with unexpected pleasure as the drift of his fingertip filled her with a curling sense of warmth which made her knees buckle.

He was famous for his restraint. For his ability to pleasure a woman until she could be pleasured no more. Then and only then would he take his own release. But this time there were no thoughts of restraint or finesse or of demonstration of his consummate skill as a lover. This time he would not wait. He groaned again as he tugged at the silken tie of his trousers. *Could* not wait.

Somehow she had fallen backwards onto the bed, on top of her discarded clothes which had been lying there, but none of that seemed to matter. Nothing mattered other than the sight of her dark and golden and fiercely aroused lover as he prepared to straddle her, and a sigh caught painfully in her throat.

Rashid! Her beautiful, beloved Rashid! Hers, but never really hers. Not now. Only this once. She felt the threat of tears pricking at her eyes. She wanted him. Needed him. She always had done. And just for once she would taste the pleasures of paradise in his arms. She opened her eyes and her arms to him in silent invitation though her heart felt as if it was breaking.

For with that look of raw, ill-concealed passion on his face it was so very easy to imagine that she loved him still. She made a little moan of regret and longing, and her fingertips met the rasp of his shadowed chin. He bent his head to kiss her again, and that kiss swept her away into a world that she could barely believe existed.

He moved over her, so aroused that he could barely contain himself. What had she done to him? This vixen! This desert cat! This wicked, wanton and unknown Jenna who had taken another to her bed! He lifted his mouth away from hers and bent his head to briefly suckle her breast, felt the knife-edge of bitterness as he thought of what she had thrown away. She could have suckled his baby, he thought. That joy could have been hers. And his.

But then his thoughts were overtaken by a need to possess her. A need so strong and so urgent that he was eaten up by it. Her eyes were wide and her lips were parted in gleaming invitation as he entered her.

And when she let out a stifled cry he thought at first it was because he was so big inside her. By the desert flower, he had never *felt* so big! But something warned him that this was not all as it seemed. The little tremor as her nails bit into his shoulders—as if what was happening was new to her.

He stared down at her in disbelief, watching the tears begin to slide from beneath the corners of her tightly closed eyes, and it hit him like a body-blow just what was happening.

He tried to stop himself, but it was too late for that—far too late. He felt the slow shuddering of an orgasm so deep and intense and earth-shattering that he thought he might die at that very moment, and be happy to die that way.

For a moment the world lost meaning as it shifted out of focus, and then reality began to creep back, like the first faint sun after the winter freeze.

He stifled a groan, and when he had stilled he withdrew from her as gently as he could. But he did not need to see the scarlet flowering which had spread over the clothes and divan like new blossom. He had guessed for himself.

He caught her against his bare chest. But she was stiff and unmoving in his arms as the words caught in his throat like dust and his heart pounded with something very close to pain.

'You were a virgin,' he said flatly.

CHAPTER FIVE

JENNA didn't answer for a moment, but when she opened her eyes it was to surprise an expression of something approaching sorrow in his own. Moving out of his embrace, she reached for the huge towel which lay beside the bed and cuddled it over her protectively, though its warmth did little to take the edge off her feeling of naked exposure and her teeth began to chatter violently.

'*Weren't* you, Jenna?' he demanded again, but this time his voice was gentler. 'A virgin?'

'Y-yes,' she stumbled.

'You lied to me,' he said, but it was less an accusation and more as though he was trying to work out some kind of insoluble calculation.

She bit down on her lip. 'Yes, again.'

There was a heartbeat of a pause. 'But I don't understand.' His voice sounded dazed. 'I don't understand why.'

It was the closest she had ever heard to Rashid admitting confusion. She opened her eyes and wished that she hadn't, for he was lying on his side, leaning on his elbow with his chin resting on his hand. And, although his eyes burned into her with their jet-dark question, he seemed thoroughly unselfconscious in his nakedness.

His body was burnished gold by the sunlight which filtered in through the shutters, as if he had been moulded from some precious metal. It was a very, very beautiful body, thought Jenna.

But it had not brought her pleasure, she reminded herself achingly—and now it never would.

'Why, Jenna?' he persisted, and his eyes narrowed as he saw the sudden tremble of her lips. He who had never failed a woman had failed this one!

44

She shook her head. 'I can't,' she whispered. 'I'm not having this conversation now. Not here. Like this.' Beneath the towel she felt more vulnerable still, worried that he might touch her again—and even more stupidly worried that he would not. How had this unthinkable situation come about? 'I'd l-like to get dressed, please.'

He narrowed his eyes, and then nodded. 'Go and get dressed, then,' he said quietly. 'But I'm not going anywhere.'

She edged him a pleading look as she moved off the bed with as much dignity as she could muster.

But he ignored her silent request. He obviously had no intention of moving. True to his word, he continued to lie there, as lazily indolent as a cat who had just sampled a particularly large saucer of cream. Couldn't he just do the decent thing, and go—and leave her with this terrible sense of regret?

She grabbed her underwear and her silky Quador clothes and, feeling his dark eyes still on her body, moved towards the bathroom, where she defiantly turned the key in the door very loudly.

She showered for a long time, washing every last musky trace of his masculine scent from her body, and then she slipped on the robes, which were coloured palest blue, and went back into the room, expecting—no, hoping—that he would be gone.

But he had not gone. Of course he hadn't.

Some time during her shower he had put his own robes back on, and now he was sprawled, silent and watchful, on one of the long, low couches which lay beneath the window.

His lashes concealed the expression in his shuttered eyes, and his face had never looked more impossibly remote as he followed her movements.

Rashid watched her. Her body was completely and decently covered now, but she still exuded an irresistible sensuality. A sensuality which had made him weak as he had never been weak before!

His mouth tightened. 'I think you owe me some kind of explanation, Jenna.'

'I owe you nothing!' she retorted hotly. Not now. She had paid her dues in full.

A glimmer of humour—the very first she had seen since she had walked into his palace that day—briefly softened the hard, dark eyes. 'You like to fight with me, don't you?' he observed softly.

She shook her head. 'No one ever fights with you.'

'You do,' he contradicted. 'Jenna.' His deep voice lingered on the syllables and made it sound like an erotic entreaty. 'Why did you tell me that you had had a lover when it is now self-evident that there has been no one?'

Except for you, she thought, with sad bitterness. And in the end she had blown it, so caught up with nerves as he had entered her that she had known no pleasure at all.

'Do you really need to know?' she asked wearily.

'Yes.'

She guessed that there was no point in evading this particular issue. What Rashid wanted, Rashid generally got—and why shouldn't he know the truth?

'It was a last desperate attempt to get out of marrying you,' she said.

He frowned as if had misheard her. *'Desperate?'* he echoed incredulously. 'You would go to such lengths not to marry me?'

'That's right.' She nodded her head, spurred on by a determination that he should know the strength of her resolve. 'I don't want to marry you, be your wife. I told you that repeatedly, Rashid but, as usual, you wouldn't listen! You ordered me over here in spite of my objections. You want your own sweet way and you're determined to get it—just like you always do!'

'You flatter me, Jenna,' he said sarcastically.

'No, I don't—and what is more I never will! Everyone else around here does, and that's half your trouble!'

'Half my trouble?' he repeated dangerously. 'And just what is *that* supposed to mean?'

'That you're arrogant!' she offered.

Black brows were raised in imperious question, as if she had just rather stupidly stated the obvious. 'And?'

His lazy acknowledgement filled her with the courage to tell him what was really going on in her mind. 'And I don't want to marry an arrogant man! I don't want the kind of marriage you are offering me!' she declared. She saw him open his mouth to object, but she shook her head and carried on, not caring that no one *ever* interrupted Rashid! 'When I get married, I want it to be as an equal!'

'An equal?' he repeated faintly.

'Yes! It's an interesting word, isn't it, Rashid? One which I learnt in America! Go and look it up in the dictionary if you really don't understand it!'

'I think you forget yourself!' he said tightly.

'I think not!' she contradicted, and for a moment her vulnerability and sense of regret were washed away by an overwhelming wave of *power*! She was no longer bound by an ancient promise to him! She was free to say exactly as she pleased—and maybe some long-overdue home truths wouldn't go amiss.

'I don't want the kind of marriage your parents had. All Quador men consider it to be their unquestionable right to...' She clamped her lips together firmly.

'To what, Jenna?' he questioned silkily.

As if he needed telling! She shivered with distaste. 'To have mistresses!'

'Mistresses?'

Her pent-up anger and frustration exploded in a fit of temper she hadn't seen in herself for a long, long time. 'Oh, please don't insult my intelligence by playing dumb with me, Rashid!' she snapped. 'I'm not stupid, and neither is everyone else! I read the newspapers, you know!'

He noticed the ragged breathing which was making her delightful breasts rise up and down quite enticingly, and thought fleetingly that if it had been any other woman he might have taken her straight back to bed there and then.

But then if it had been any other woman he doubted he would have lost all control and left her unsatisfied. A fact which was surely contributing to her magnificent temper—a temper which was making her look fiery and beautiful and almost *formidable*.

Neither men nor women lost their temper in front of him, and in this woman the novelty value was proving highly erotic. But enough was enough; she needed to know who was the master.

'Explain yourself!' he commanded.

Jenna pursed her lips together. 'The whole world knows that you have many women,' she began, and when she saw the slight shrugging of his shoulders her blood pressure threatened to shoot through the ceiling. 'You see! There you go again! Looking as though it's something to be *proud* of!'

'Many men do it,' he commented quietly. 'But mostly they don't have the paparazzi waiting around to capture the moment on film!'

She sucked in a breath of outrage that was directed as much against her *own* behaviour as his. How could she have just let him have sex with her like that? How *could* she?

'Even in yesterday's newspaper in New York I saw that you had been pictured leaving your *friend's* apartment in Paris only the day before!' she raged. 'Cutting it a little fine, weren't you, Rashid? You must have some stamina—to have made love to her and then to come back to repeat the experience with me!'

He was contemplating giving her an insight into the *real* extent of his stamina, when he saw the faint glimmer of tears which had turned her eyes into liquid gold and he cursed aloud. What right had he to make any kind of boast in view of what had just happened?

His voice was as soft as she had ever heard it, and it soothed her as if it were a lullaby. 'I had not intended to make love to you today!' he murmured. 'As my bride, you would have come to me a virgin—and I would have been so much slower with you. So much more gentle! And now I have ruined your first experience of making love.'

'Maybe we both ruined it,' she argued quietly, and then

turned her eyes up to his. 'Oh, why did you have to follow me here, Rashid? Why didn't you just leave me alone?'

Not follow her? Rashid shook his head. His anger and his desire for her had reached a point of total combustion that could not have been denied. He hadn't asked himself what had guided him so inexorably towards her room because he had been eaten up with a gnawing kind of jealousy which had blinded him to all thought and reason.

Until he had walked into this bedchamber and seen her wrapped into nothing but a towel. And then a primitive hunger had taken over completely.

'But I could not let you go just like that,' he declared heatedly.

'Why not?'

'And let you take your leave of me with those your final words?' His question was incredulous. 'That you, as my betrothed, had taken another lover?'

She bit back the obvious remark that he had not *acted* like her betrothed for the past few years—that might smack of desperation of a different kind. And, whatever else happened today, Rashid would remember her as having some kind of innate pride.

'But there remains a question, Jenna,' he continued quietly. His deep voice sounded reflective, though the hooded black eyes told her precisely nothing of his true feelings. 'Just what do we do next?'

She stared at him, then shrugged. 'As planned,' she said steadily, 'I would like a car to take me to my father's house, please.'

His lips compressed together and he threw her a look of impatience. 'As if this had never happened?'

'I think that is probably best, under the circumstances.'

'Best?' He gave a short, hollow laugh, and then spoke in a low, urgent tone. 'I think that you must be talking out of the back of your head—as you say in America—if you think that this matter can now be forgotten.'

There was a steely determination underpinning his voice

which made her regard him with wary eyes. 'Just what do you mean by that, Rashid?' she whispered.

'I have taken your honour,' he said simply. 'Taken it in a way which grieves me bitterly to think of, and there is a price to be paid for that action.'

A price to be paid. He made it sound as if she were a diamond on sale and up for the highest bidder! 'Don't be ridiculous—'

'I am *never* ridiculous!' he lashed back, and then drew a deep, laboured breath. 'Jenna, you were always intended to be my bride, and that situation will still stand. For how can I send you home to your father, knowing what has happened between us?'

'But he need never know!' she protested, desperate now.

There was an infinitesimal pause. 'Not even if there is a baby on the way?'

Her heart missed a beat. 'A baby?' she whispered hoarsely. 'A *baby*?'

'Well, of *course* there could be a baby!' he exploded impatiently. 'Did you not learn biology at school? I used no form of contraception—and I assume that, as a virgin, you were not protected either!'

The repercussions of what they had just done began to seep into her consciousness, like blood falling onto a stone. And it hurt. 'Do you normally go around taking the risk of impregnating a woman?' she questioned huskily, but her hands were shaking as she imagined him with other women. 'Don't you ever take any responsibility for your lovemaking? Just exactly how many children have you sired—?'

'*Jenna!*' he thundered. 'I have never, ever spilled my seed into a woman before today! The royal blood of Quador cannot be squandered in such a way!'

'Then what was so different about this time?'

A pulse beat relentlessly at his temple. This he could not answer—except to tell himself that he had been out of control in a way which was completely alien to him and had shown him a side of his nature he had not known existed.

'I have no need to explain my actions to you, Jenna,' he

said softly, his eyes as hard and as bright as diamonds. 'But I see no need why the marriage should not now go ahead, as planned.'

'Couldn't we just wait to see if there's a baby on the way?' she beseeched him, knowing in her heart that it was useless, for she recognised that steely determination of old. 'And if there isn't—then couldn't we forget the whole thing?'

He knitted his dark brows together in recognition of her sustained reluctance to be his bride. 'No,' he said flatly. 'We cannot.'

'And if I refuse?'

No one refused him anything. Ever. And whether he got what he wanted by negotiation or coercion—he always won in the end. 'Perhaps you wish that I should inform your father of what has just occurred?'

Warning bells threatened to deafen her, and all she could see was the cold ebony light gleaming from his eyes. 'Rashid! You w-wouldn't d-do that!' she breathed.

'Wouldn't I?' He smiled, but the smile sent a shiver down her spine. 'Oh, I would, Jenna—believe me, I would.' The eyes glittered again. 'And what do you suspect your father would say if I told him?'

Jenna flinched. She knew very well what he would say. And feel. For a Quador man, her father was remarkably in touch with his feelings. Unlike this beast of a lion who sat so mockingly before her now! He would be hurt and angry that she had lost her honour before her marriage. He would feel her to be compromised, as indeed she now was. Quador had such black and white views on a subject like this, she thought. Oh, why had she ever agreed to come back?

'He would make me marry you,' she said woodenly. 'You know he would.'

'Correction. He would be *delighted* for you to marry me. It was always what he wanted.'

She shook her shorn head distractedly. How *could* her father, her sweet gentle father, possibly have agreed to let his daughter be given to this...this...? 'Barbarian!' she spat at him.

He gave a low laugh. 'Oh, how I enjoy your protestations and your defiance, Jenna,' he murmured. 'Your capitulation will make a worthy prize, and you, my sweet, will make a most stimulating partner!'

Defensively, she locked her long fingers around her neck. 'Partner!' she echoed. 'I can't believe you have the nerve to use an expression which describes some kind of *sharing*!'

'We will share many things,' he promised. 'And I will show you how much lovemaking *can* be enjoyed.'

She felt sick.

Sex.

That was what this was all about. Sex and pride and blood-lines and showing her just why he was considered one of the world's greatest lovers. Whatever had happened to the mention of love? But more fool her for wishing for the impossible. It had never been anything other than a business arrangement, and one which he had been happy to avoid for as long as possible.

And when he tired of her, as he inevitably would, what then? For Rashid had known many women in his life—why on earth should he settle for a life of marital fidelity when he was used to variety in the most exotic sense imaginable.

Could she bear it? She imagined some not-too-distant day when he would go abroad on 'business'—but in reality would no doubt be seeking out the experienced warmth of Chantal, or women just like her?

But what else could she do?

She asked herself what alternative she had, tried to imagine the scenario of thwarting his wishes and risking her father's wrath. She thought of Nadia, too—and her loving but clandestine relationship with Brad. What if Rashid followed her back to New York, determined to get his own way, and discovered the truth about her sister and her American lover, as doubtless he would?

He would put a stop to *that*, as well—she wouldn't put it past him. And how could she threaten her dear sister's very obvious happiness because of a bizarre sequence of events which had culminated in her losing her innocence to Rashid?

She had no choice—she was doomed if she did and doomed if she didn't. Her fevered mind could not see any alternative to the one which lay so darkly in front her.

She nodded her head, her face full of resignation, but she did not flinch from his piercing gaze. 'You may take me as your bride, Rashid,' she said, with quiet dignity. 'But you cannot make me a willing partner! And here is something else that might make you change your mind—I will never enjoy sex with you. Never, ever, *ever*!'

By the shafts of his silken-clad thighs he clenched his fists with anger, but only for a moment. He must maintain control—at least until after the ceremony. But it wasn't easy—not with her lips parted in protest and just begging to be kissed.

Resisting the urge to crush her into his arms and to prove her wrong in the most unequivocal way possible, he stood up and towered over her, like some dark, avenging statue.

'You must know that I like nothing better than a challenge, my impetuous Jenna,' he said softly. 'How I will take pleasure in making you take those words back, in having you sigh my name over and over again as you beg for more, and yet more.'

'Never!' she said again, but that look of dark intent in his eyes was difficult to challenge.

'We shall see,' came his cool retort. 'Now, come. Let us go to your father. Let us break the happy news to him.'

CHAPTER SIX

'YOUR Sheikh awaits you, mistress. The wedding draws near.'

The words seemed to come at her from a long way away, and Jenna forced herself back into the present from out of the wistful thoughts which had occupied her mind for much of the last week. And one thought alone had dominated.

There was to be no baby.

The discovery had not surprised her, for physically she had not felt any different—and surely she would have felt profoundly and completely different if Rashid's child had been growing inside her womb?

But she had been unprepared for the primitive swamping of despondency when she had learned that she would not start her married life as a pregnant woman. At least a baby would have given her some reason for being. Some *reason* for being married to a man who did not love her.

She had spent sleepless nights weeping silently into her pillow as she mourned something which all common-sense told her was the best thing which could have happened.

Yet Rashid, too, had not reacted as she might have expected. There had been none of the expected exultation and relief. She had quietly told him and he had taken the news in silence, his dark eyes hooded, and then he had nodded his dark head.

'It is as destiny wills it,' he had said, his voice sounding cold and toneless.

Yet wouldn't a pregnancy have reassured him that his all-important bloodline would continue? Wasn't her fertility the most vital aspect of this union?

'Mistress,' said her lady-in-waiting again. 'Your Sheikh awaits you.'

Jenna stared into the floor-length mirror as if scarcely believing the image which was projected back at her.

She did indeed look fit for a king!

She wore a heavy gold satin gown, richly and lavishly studded with jewels, which weighed almost as much as she did. Her hair had grown a little in the weeks leading up to the wedding. Rashid had not demanded it—he had not needed to. She had seen the unmistakable glitter of disapproval every time those dark eyes had surveyed her long, bare neck. Quador women wore their hair long—and now that she was the public representative of those women she would have to do the same. And, in truth, she had missed the weight and the silken caress of her waist-length locks.

Today, her hair was adorned with tiny jewelled clips—and every jewel was the real McCoy. She was wearing a king's ransom on her head!

Diamonds. Sapphires. Rubies and emeralds. All gleamed with multi-coloured splendour—dazzling and bright—making her face look pale by comparison. Her amber eyes glittered back at her, huge and haunted and distracted, and the fingers which were clasped together by the heavily encrusted belt which lay low over her hips were trembling like the first leaves of spring.

And no wonder. For the day she had so been dreading had finally arrived.

Her wedding day.

For the past forty-eight hours world leaders had been flying into Riocard, as had film stars and models and moguls—rich and powerful friends and acquaintances of the man who seemed like a cold-faced stranger to her.

The world's press were camped along the wedding route and glossy magazines from just about every country in the world had been sent to cover the 'wedding of the year'. She had received countless requests for interviews, but she had refused them all—for surely perceptive journalists would easily be able to detect her uncertainty. And her insecurity about the future.

From outside she could hear the sounds of the jubilant crowds lining the main streets of Riocard, in the hope of catching a glimpse of their Sheikh's bride as she travelled with her father to the palace for the ceremony which would make them man and wife.

Rashid's wife.

Jenna shivered, trying not to think about what lay ahead. First there was the ceremony itself—with all the eyes of Quador on her, along with the eyes of the world. They would be expecting a bride who was rapturous with joy at the thought of marrying one of the world's most eligible bachelors.

She allowed herself a wry smile. If only they knew! What would they say if they discovered that she and Rashid had barely spoken a word to each other in the intervening weeks— let alone loving words. They had discussed only what had been absolutely necessary.

Only once, with her father in proud attendance, had she summoned up the courage to ask Rashid about what her future 'role' as his wife would entail.

And Rashid had narrowed his black eyes and fixed her with a look of bemused tolerance.

'Why, Jenna,' he had responded softly, 'your role is to support your Sheikh.'

'But I have been studying law, Rashid,' she had pointed out. 'Could that not be put to some use?'

Her father had shaken his head and smiled. 'Your role as consort will leave you little spare time, Jenna.'

And Rashid, murmuring his agreement, had risen, his silken robes flowing, signalling that the discussion had come to an end.

The chaperons had put paid to all but the most formal communication between them. Like questions from Rashid about her preferences for the wedding feast—and, on one memorable occasion, a drawled query about where she would care to spend the honeymoon.

As far away from you as possible, her eyes had said, but she had given him a sarcastically submissive smile. 'That choice must be yours, O Sheikh,' she had answered softly, and had seen his mouth tighten in response. 'Perhaps Paris?' she had questioned, with mock innocence. 'I believe that the Sheikh knows the city *very* well?'

He had drummed his long fingers on the exquisite inlaid

desk at which he'd sat, and his dark eyes had frosted her a look of pure ice.

'Perhaps we should stay right here in Quador,' he had murmured in a little-spoken Quadorian dialect which he knew full well that she alone in the room understood. 'After all—one bed is pretty much the same as any other!'

Jenna shivered again. After the wedding and the feast would come the wedding night itself, and that was the part she was dreading most. She had declared that she would not respond to him, that she would tolerate his caresses but not enjoy them. Yet over the last few headachy days she had begun to wonder whether she would have the resolve to withstand his raw and heated sensuality.

But even if she didn't there was no guarantee that she would enjoy it—not if that single, frantic bout in the bedchamber was anything to go by. And if she was worried that Rashid would be unable to resist the lure of mistresses past, present and maybe future—then she was almost certain that a frigid wife would send him running straight to their beds.

She stared into the mirror one last time and fixed a practised smile onto her lips. She would go forward towards her future, and put her trust in fate.

There was little else in which she could trust.

Rashid stood with narrowed eyes as he surveyed the horizon for the first sign of her carriage.

'Exalted One?'

Rashid didn't move, his heart unaccustomedly heavy. 'What is it, Abdullah?'

'The woman—Chantal—she has been leaving messages for you, O Sheikh.'

Rashid *did* turn round then, his narrowed eyes growing even more flinty than usual. 'You dare to speak to me of such matters on the day of my wedding?'

'I merely pass on messages, Sheikh, just as I have always done.'

'Then pass them on no longer,' said Rashid tonelessly. 'I instructed Chantal not to contact me. She knows that I am a man of my word.'

'Indeed.' Abdullah nodded.

'Did she choose one of the pieces of jewellery I left?' Rashid enquired, as an afterthought.

Abdullah shifted uncomfortably. 'She said that making a choice was impossible, Excellency.'

'And?'

'She kept them all.'

For a moment the Sheikh was still, and then he smiled a cynical smile. 'So be it,' he murmured. 'Then there is nothing more to be said.' He stilled once more as bells began pealing loudly in the palace courtyard. 'She is here,' he breathed. 'Jenna has come.'

Moving stiffly in the heavy wedding gown, and surrounded by her women-in-waiting, Jenna made her way slowly towards the Throne Room, where Rashid awaited her.

And with her first glimpse of him a small, instinctive sigh escaped from her lips—for he looked as perfect as it was surely possible for any man to look.

He wore robes of silver, far plainer than her own, and from his belt hung the priceless Quador sword which was never far from his side. He turned around and his carved face was stern, but for one brief moment the dark eyes softened as he bowed his head with imperial grace.

He had got what he wanted, she thought as she moved across the crowded ornate room to his side—while her own wishes had been cast aside in the tide of his arrogant determination.

'You look exquisite,' he murmured.

And so did he. She bowed her own head, because, stupidly, the appreciative blaze from the black eyes had made it seem like the most wonderful compliment she had ever received. A tiny morsel thrown to a starving dog. 'Thank you.'

The ceremony passed in a blur. Ancient words were spoken. Heavy crowns placed upon their heads. The wedding vows were quietly made—vows of love and endurance and fidelity. And, staring into the onyx glitter of his eyes, Jenna found the words all too simple to say. A wave of sadness rocked her, for she *had* loved him with all her heart, and deep down she suspected that she still could.

But as Rashid echoed her words of undying fidelity they sounded hollow and empty in her ears.

He placed a circlet of rubies on her finger as the words of the ceremony echoed around the high-vaulted Throne Room.

They were married. Man and wife. Jenna felt faint as her eyes were drawn to a sudden cloud-like spectacle outside the window—the blur of wings as a thousand white doves were released into the skies.

How free they looked, she thought wistfully. How carefree.

Rashid felt her tremble beside him as she watched the birds fly away. 'What troubles you, Jenna?' he whispered.

He did. She turned to face him, her brow criss-crossing with concern. 'Will the doves not fly straight into the desert and perish?' she questioned worriedly.

He gave a brief, hard smile. Did she think so badly of him? 'I am not such a barbarian as to condemn such living beauty to death,' he demurred. 'No, they will be carried on the warm thermals to more hospitable climes than Quador. Who knows? They may settle where no dove has ever settled before—a new beginning for them as well as for us, sweet Jenna.'

Jenna suppressed a sigh of longing. He could make his words sound like poetry—if only he meant them!

After the wedding came the feast in the Banqueting Hall, and there were murmurs of approval from the glittering assembly as they looked around, observing for themselves the vast wealth of Quador.

Meats were turning on vast spits. Huge bowls of jewel-bright and glistening fruits tempted the eye and the palate. But Jenna had little appetite for food and she felt dazed in the spotlight of so many curious stares.

She drank some strong wine from one of the carved golden goblets, and the fiery liquid burned into her stomach, filling her with a welcome warmth.

Rashid bent his head to her ear. 'And now we must move into the Grand Ballroom, my sweet bride,' he murmured softly. 'They are awaiting our first dance.'

'Duty calls,' she responded with a nod of her head, and the thumping in her head only increased as she saw him frown.

A string quartet had been flown in from New York and they played quietly in one corner of the ballroom as Jenna moved into her new husband's arms.

For a moment she saw the envious eyes of an international starlet fixed on them—a woman whose tiny, glittering dress showed off every perfect inch of her body. And then she was aware of nothing other than the scent of the man who was now her husband, and the lean, hard body beneath the fine silk he wore.

He touched his lips to her ear, and she shivered. 'You are pale, Jenna mine,' he observed. 'Has your wedding day not pleased you?'

She lifted her head up, dazzled by the piercing black light from his eyes. 'It has all been so…bewildering,' she said truthfully. 'I hadn't thought…hadn't realised just what a big show it was going to be.'

His eyes narrowed. *'Show?'* he questioned, his voice sultry, but underlaid with a faint note of impatience. 'The trappings are necessary, but a wedding is a wedding is a wedding—and tonight I will show you just how fulfilling married life can be.'

She quickly turned her face into his shoulder again, for fear that he should see the foreboding in her eyes.

Rashid felt the stiff tension in her body, but kept his face relaxed, knowing that every eye in the room was on them, and that every nuance would be observed and reported back.

What had happened to the easy warmth which had once flowed like honey between them? Should he ever have let her leave? Was he to blame for this frosty state of impasse? He allowed himself a small sigh. He bitterly regretted the way he had taken her, with such fervour and such little consideration for her innocence. He had believed her rash declaration. Had thought that she was a woman of sexual experience—and oh, how wrong he had been.

He drifted his mouth to the jewelled hair, remembering her angry words to him. So she would not enjoy sex! He smiled. Let her say that when the morning sun washed its first golden rays over their naked bodies!

It was almost eight by the time they took their leave of their guests. They were to spend that night in the Palace, before travelling to the west of Quador the following day, where Rashid had a hunting lodge and only a bare skeleton of servants.

They would be almost alone, she realised—or as alone as a man in his position could ever be.

'Come now, Jenna,' he said softly, and, taking her hand, he led her past the clapping guests towards his quarters. 'Let the wedding night begin.'

It was a journey which seemed to take for ever, and all Jenna was aware of was the pounding of her heart and the powerful presence of the silver-clad Sheikh by her side as they mounted the marble stairs.

At last he drew her inside the door of a room which was indisputably the room of the Ruler. The floors were also of marble, and priceless paintings of his ancestors clothed the walls. At the far end, looking almost a car journey away, stood the wide, low divan—hung with embroidered canopies, a coverlet of pure gold silk spread smoothly across its surface.

He could feel her trembling as he turned her to face him, and he stared down for a long moment into her heart-shaped upturned face.

'Do not be afraid, Jenna,' he murmured. 'For you have nothing to fear.'

Save for her own shortcomings and being at the mercy of a man who knew everything there was to know about the art of love, while she knew almost nothing.

He began to draw the tiny jewelled clips from her hair almost absently, and placed them on an inlaid table. The style was far less severe now, he thought, and framed her face with soft waves of silky golden-brown.

He bent his lips to hers and for a moment she tensed, but the brush of his mouth was as light and as drifting as a feather, and it was barely there before it was gone again.

Rashid sighed. 'You look as though you are just about to enter the lion's den,' he observed.

She felt a smile wobble its way across her mouth. 'How very appropriate,' she observed drily. 'Since you are known as the Lion of the Desert!'

He laughed, and the white teeth gleamed in such contrast against the olive skin, and Jenna was startled by how long it had been since she had seen him laugh like that.

He tipped her chin upwards and looked down into her eyes. 'You are tired,' he commented wryly, and took her hand to lead her to the divan. 'Come, let me undress you, and then you shall sleep.'

'Sleep, Rashid?' she echoed disbelievingly, and saw him knit the dark brows together.

'Believe it or not, I am not the barbarian you once called me,' he responded coolly. 'Perhaps you have reason to fear my advances—presumably that is why you vowed never to enjoy sex. I will not force myself upon you, and neither will I beg you, Jenna,' he asserted softly. 'You will come to me willing, or you will not come at all. There will be no demands made on you which you do not wish to fulfil.'

Now she felt utterly confused. He began to deftly undo all the tiny buttons which adorned the front of her wedding gown, and his words set up a nagging feeling of doubt and insecurity. What did he mean? It was his right as her Sheikh and her husband to consummate the marriage, surely?

She threw him a look of challenge. 'I feel as though I could sleep for a week,' she admitted.

'Then so be it.' The last of the buttons was freed and he helped her step from the heavy dress, sucking in an instinctive breath as he saw what she was wearing. For the gown might be traditional Quadorian, but the undergarments beneath were sheer Hollywood.

An underwired bra in fine gold lace—which curved her breasts upwards into two exquisitely pale mounds—and an outrageous G-string in matching material which emphasised the darker triangular shadowing which blurred so tantalisingly before his eyes.

'Who bought these?' he questioned unsteadily.

She lifted her eyes to his. 'My ladies-in-waiting instructed me to be beautiful for my wedding night. I sent to… to…America for them.'

And beautiful she most certainly was—but the haunted look

in her eyes was no spur to making love to her. He turned away abruptly, afraid that the reined-in control he could feel tightening his face would only add to her trepidation.

'Get into bed,' he said, more harshly than he had intended, and went to stand by the window.

She did as he instructed, and some of her apprehensiveness was relieved the moment her body sank into the welcome softness of the divan. She stretched beneath the coverlet, and the tension began to seep away.

She was here and she was Rashid's wife, waiting in his bed, and the doubts which had nagged her all day suddenly crystallised into certainty. Had he not just been gentle and considerate with her? And would she not fulfil her own worst fears if she held him at arm's length? Wouldn't that almost certainly drive him into the arms of another woman?

From beneath her long lashes, she stole a look at him. His lean physique exuded the same kind of restrained power as a caged tiger, and a tiny throb of aching warmth made her limbs feel suddenly fluid.

'Rashid?' she questioned tentatively.

He turned around, but his face was so impassive that it appeared almost indifferent.

'I am going to take a shower,' he stated.

Jenna nodded, and swallowed down another doubt. Shouldn't she have bathed herself? Come to her Sheikh scented and shining? For one mad and impetuous moment she opened her mouth, about to offer to wash his back, just like a modern, liberated woman.

Except she must remember that she was not—that her independence had only ever been an illusion. And besides, he had already stalked off into the bathroom and banged the door behind him.

Rashid stripped off his wedding clothes with a grim and ruthless efficiency and turned the shower on full, standing beneath it for long, countless moments.

When he returned, with only some of his ardour dampened by the cool jets of water, she was fast asleep.

CHAPTER SEVEN

JENNA awoke late the next morning, blinking her eyes in confusion as her sleep-befuddled mind struggled to work out exactly where she was, and when she did her eyes flew open.

In Rashid's bed.

His wife!

Slowly she turned her face to the empty space beside her, and saw that the pillow lay as smooth and as untouched as it had the night before.

'Fear not, my beauty,' came a mocking voice from what seemed like a long way away, and she narrowed her eyes to look at the far end of the room, where Rashid stood like an imposing statue suddenly brought to life as he began to walk towards her.

He was fully dressed in silken robes of creamy buttermilk, against which his dark and golden looks appeared all the more startling. But his face was hard and impenetrable, with a certain edge to it, and there was nothing of the appearance of the eager groom about him.

Her hand flew to her heart, feeling its wild fluttering as he continued to walk towards the bed. 'Rashid,' she said breathlessly, 'you are up very early.'

He made a small murmur of dissent. 'It is almost ten, Jenna—and soon the sun will be high in the sky. We must make haste for the lodge before that happens.'

She had to know. She *had* to. 'Where did you...where did you—?'

'Sleep?' he interrupted, his dark eyes flashing with cruel humour. 'Why, I slept on the divan beneath the window, Jenna—for fear of disturbing your sleep.'

Beneath the silk coverlet her body trembled, her other hand moving towards her breasts. She was still wearing her fancy bridal underwear, she realised, her cheeks growing pink. She must have fallen asleep without remembering to take it off.

And Rashid had not removed it either—in fact he had not wanted even to share a bed with her. What she had been half-dreading and half-longing for had failed to materialise, and yet the fact gave her not one moment of pleasure. Better that he should have ravished her than treat her this morning with such insulting indifference!

She forced herself to meet the mocking black light of his eyes. 'There was room for two, Rashid,' she said quietly. 'You didn't have to sleep over there and be uncomfortable all night.'

'On the contrary,' he responded coolly. 'It was not in the least bit uncomfortable.' He hadn't achieved much sleep, all the same—but he suspected that it was more than he would have gained if he had subjected himself to the torture of lying beside her sleeping body without touching her.

'Oh. Well, I'm glad you had a good night's sleep,' she said, rather woodenly.

He allowed the faint drift of a smile to glimmer at the corners of his mouth. 'That wasn't what I said at all,' he offered obliquely. 'But you certainly did, didn't you?'

She nodded. 'Yes. I was very tired.'

Or just eager to lose herself in the safety net of sleep? His mouth tightened. 'Now get dressed, Jenna, and we will leave as soon as you are ready.'

She waited until he had left the room and then distractedly showered and put on silk trousers and a slim-fitting matching tunic, which were more suited to travelling along the bumpy roads to the lodge than one of the more formal and elaborate outfits which comprised her trousseau.

When she went downstairs to where he was breakfasting a sudden dark gleam of approval softened the hard eyes and he motioned for her to come and sit beside him.

He poured her coffee and handed her a dish of fruit, and his hand suddenly reached out to trace the skin beneath her eyes.

'All those dark shadows gone,' he observed quietly.

'Yes.' The shadows beneath her eyes were only being replaced by the shadows in her heart. But the tender gesture disarmed her, and Jenna found herself smiling in response before tucking into the exotic fruits with something approaching her normal appetite.

He refilled her coffee cup and she found herself relaxing. Yet his consideration and his restraint both charmed and alarmed her. This Rashid was more like the Rashid of old, she thought—and that was dangerous. For he was not the same man at all. The Rashid she had loved had been the ideal fantasy man of her dreams. The perfect man and the perfect lover—forsaking all others and loyal only to her.

But the true man had been as much of an illusion as her own hard-fought-for independence. And if a man like Rashid had known many pleasures of the flesh—then how long before he was tempted into tasting them again?

Especially a man who had not even spent his wedding night in the same bed as his wife...

She pushed her cup away and looked up to find him watching her.

'Shall we leave immediately?' he questioned softly.

Jenna nodded. 'As you wish.'

Outside stood a gleaming four-wheel drive, and Jenna's mouth curved into an instinctive smile. 'No ancient Quador chariot, this,' she observed.

'You don't approve?' he murmured.

'Of course I approve! I know only too well how treacherous the unmade roads can be! It's just that in America these vehicles are used on suburban school-runs—I'm sure that many of my friends over there would be surprised to learn that it is also the honeymoon car of the Sheikh and his wife!'

He narrowed his eyes. 'You mean that they wouldn't think it romantic enough?' he mused.

'Possibly.'

His eyes glinted. 'But comfort can be very romantic, Jenna—as you shall discover for yourself when you let me escort you in air-conditioned splendour!'

He was right, it *was* romantic. Beguilingly and misleadingly so.

Closeted together on the back seat, speeding through the sweetly familiar countryside, it felt almost like old times. They passed places where he had taken her riding as a child, and the past somehow became inextricably bound up in the confusing state of the present.

The child in her had dreamed of a moment such as this, and yet the woman she had become seemed less certain of anything than the child had been.

He watched the play of emotions which chased over her face as they drove deeper and deeper into Quador, forcing himself not to take her into his arms and kiss away all the barriers between them. She would come to *him* or not at all, he reminded himself grimly.

'Will you miss America?' he asked suddenly.

She turned to face him. His dark handsome face sent a spear of longing through her, surprised by an unfamiliar look of disquiet there.

She shrugged her shoulders a little. 'I thought I would,' she admitted. 'But this is home—and home occupies a part of your heart that no other place ever can.'

'That is a good start,' he mused. 'For a honeymoon.'

But what kind of honeymoon? she wondered as the car bumped along an unmade track to the hunting lodge she had not visited for years, and a small sigh escaped from her lips.

'What is it?' he questioned.

'I—I'd forgotten how beautiful it was,' she sighed, as the long, low building which stood in the shadow of snow-peaked mountains came into view.

And he had forgotten how beautiful *she* was—even with her magnificent hair all shorn off. He had allowed her perfect profile and those high, delicious cheekbones to fade from the forefront of his mind. He had allowed the two of them to become worlds apart. And now surely they *were* worlds apart?

'It's been a long time,' he agreed. 'Too long since I was here, also.'

'Seriously?' She squinted her eyes to look at him. 'But you used to come up here whenever possible!'

His smile was rueful. 'You think that extended breaks go hand-in-hand with ruling a country the size of Quador?'

'You don't delegate?'

'Delegate?' He gave a short laugh. 'Delegation is a luxury I can seldom afford, Jenna. Being accepted by my people means that my profile always needs to be high.'

'But you *are* accepted by your people!' she said, with sudden passion. 'You know you are, Rashid!'

He smiled. 'Careful! That sounded very nearly like a compliment!'

She laughed back, caught in the dark cross-fire of his eyes. 'Hold your horses—I wouldn't go that far!'

For a moment they shared the compatibility of days gone by, and Rashid felt his heart thunder like the pound of equine hooves. 'Speaking of horses—are you hungry?'

Hungry? How could she be hungry for anything other than the taste of his lips on hers once more? She shook her head. 'No, not a bit. I had a big breakfast. Why?'

'Then shall we ride together, Jenna? As we used to?'

There was a heartbeat of a pause, but she hid her disappointment. 'Yes, Sheikh,' she answered quietly. 'I would like that.'

The driver had come round to open the door of the car. 'Let us go inside and change,' Rashid said, and his voice had deepened.

Shown inside by a delighted servant, Jenna felt a peculiar mixture of relief and disappointment to discover that she had been allocated her own separate room, complete with a large divan and a luxurious *en suite* bathroom. She guessed that Rashid had a mirror image, only larger—and she also guessed that this meant that they could spend nights apart should they wish. She told herself that royal custom decreed it, that it had always been so and that she must just accept it.

And wasn't it easier to slither into her jodhpurs and a long-sleeved white shirt without those mocking black eyes fixed on her—reminding her that in every way that mattered this was not a *real* marriage.

But all her anxieties and fears were washed away when

Rashid led her into the stables and she was confronted by the sight of the Arab mare whose golden-brown and gleaming skin did, as Rashid had once commented, so cleverly mimic her own.

For a moment she was speechless, and then she turned to him, her eyes wide and brimming with tears which were not just about the horse. 'Pasha!' she whispered. 'Can it really be so?'

'Of course.' His voice was very soft, but his heart beat strangely as he saw the luminous amber gaze she directed at him. 'Did you think that once you had left for America I would let your father sell her to a stranger?'

Jenna put her arms around the horse and pressed her face close to its warm neck, breathing in the scent of a long-forgotten youth. 'Why, Rashid?'

'Because the horse belongs to you, Jenna, and always shall.' His voice deepened into a sultry caress. 'Just as you shall always belong to me.'

She thought that the words sounded more like a stamp of possession than any declaration of affection, but at least he wasn't seducing her with false promises. Still with her arm draped around the horse's neck, she stared into the irresistible dark glitter of his eyes. She didn't *want* to be only half a wife, she realised.

His words to her came filtering painfully back. He would not beg her, and if she came to him it must be as one who was willing.

Should that moment be now?

But the eyes of the bodyguards who stood discreetly in the shadows of the stables were upon them, and Rashid would not approve of a display of feelings in front of his staff.

Instead, unaided, she swung herself up into the saddle and flashed him a smile of challenge.

'Race you, then,' she said.

And with a small exultant laugh he mounted his own night-dark stallion with the grace of the born horseman. 'Done,' he murmured, and trotted out of the stable before she had time to gather her reins.

'Cheat!' she called after him, but her cry was lost on the desert wind. And suddenly nothing else mattered other than the pounding movement and graceful strength of the animal beneath her. The sand flew up in fine clouds from beneath Pasha's hooves and Jenna gave a whoop of sheer, unadulterated pleasure as she raced to catch her Sheikh up.

With the purity of the desert spread out before them, they rode for hours, but always within sight of the mounted bodyguards. Every now and then Rashid made them stop to drink from cool flagons of water, the sweat sheening their skin as they greedily tipped the liquid into their parched throats.

'You look happy now,' observed Rashid. Achingly, he noted a drop of water which had trickled down from her mouth and now fell with an enticing splat onto the shirt which clung to her breasts, and the heat which invaded his veins was hotter than the desert sun.

Not completely happy. But happier. She passed the flagon back to him. 'So do you,' she said softly.

'It's easy to be happy when you are unencumbered by the burdens of state,' he said wryly, with a shrug of his broad shoulders.

'If you're trying to tell me that you'd be more contented as a nomad, living out here all the time—then I would challenge you, Rashid!'

She challenged him in more ways than she would ever know. He shook his head. 'That isn't what I'm saying—I'm just making the observation that a man is the sum of many parts, and that the carefree part of me can rarely be allowed to break free.'

It was odd that he had used that word. *Carefree.* Hadn't she thought the same thing about the doves which had been released on their wedding day?

'Well, it's free enough now,' she observed mischievously. 'So why not make the most of it?' And she galloped off to the sound of his soft laughter.

The sun was sinking in the sky by the time they returned to the lodge, and the mountains had grown mysteriously darker in shades of deepest blue and green.

Jenna was uncomfortably aware of being hot and sticky and covered in dust—but even more aware of being closed in. The vast open space of the desert had guaranteed them a certain freedom and ease, but now they were inside the lodge once more the tension was back.

And how.

Rashid's face had taken on that cool, forbidding mask once more, and his words were almost clipped as he turned to her. 'Dinner will be at eight,' he told her formally. 'I will see you then.' And he turned on his heel as he headed for his own room.

Telling herself that she would *not* be disappointed by his abrupt change in attitude, she took herself off to bathe, then she slept for a while before changing for dinner. Just before eight she arrived in the dining room to find Rashid waiting for her. Her heart sank to see that his face was as darkly enigmatic as before.

It was an informal room compared to its counterpart in the palace in Riocard, but its relative simplicity did nothing to detract from the magnificent carved table and the equally magnificent chairs. It was unmistakably a royal room, made all the more so by the sight of a brooding Rashid, who was standing by a roaring log fire, for the mountain nights could be bitter.

He watched her as she walked in, all grace and sensuality in a long, white dress whose bodice was embroidered with tiny sprays of jasmine. With her face completely bare of make-up, he thought that he had never seen a woman look more lovely.

Or more untouchable—which was ironic in view of how she had behaved with him the other day. But that passionate and responsive woman seemed like a world away—and, whilst the memory filled him with the constant ache of longing, he could not deny that he was captivated by the first woman in his memory who was not using every feminine wile in the book to seduce him.

But then, why would she? She wouldn't know how to play the games of feminine seduction. She had been a *virgin*, he reminded himself with a bitter pang of guilt.

'Hello, Jenna,' he said softly.

When he looked at her like that—with a mixture of awe and hunger and fascination—she felt both shy and secure, and completely at a loss as to how to handle things. She couldn't just walk straight into his arms, could she? Especially not as a servant was bringing in a steaming platter of Quador chicken and another dish of spicy rice.

'Hello,' she said simply.

'Are you exhausted after your ride?'

She wondered whether that was a leading question. If she said that she was, then wouldn't that give him the excuse to sleep alone again? And anyway, she did not feel in the least bit tired; she felt *alive*, exhilarated—as though anything could happen on this night.

She shook her head. 'Not a bit—I'd forgotten just how relaxing riding could be.' She looked at him from between slitted lashes. 'And you?'

His smile was tight. 'I have never felt less tired in my life,' he said, his voice pure velvet.

It wasn't easy to concentrate on anything other than the dark and proud face, but she made a big effort. Somehow she forced herself to eat something, for she had eaten nothing since breakfast, and to drink the iced juice which was poured for her.

But they chatted like old times, and as some of the apprehension left her body it was replaced by the certainty of what she must now do.

Because it was up to her.

She knew that Rashid had a will of steel—and, much as she suspected that he wanted her, the first move must come from her. Her bitter words could not just be unsaid; she must show him that she was willing to be a wife to him in every sense of the word.

They had finished their coffee and the fire was very low when he lifted his dark head and fixed her with a glittering stare.

'And now, Jenna?' he questioned softly.

This definitely *was* a loaded question. Her lips felt like parchment as she stared into his dark chiselled face.

'I think it is time for bed,' she managed.

He needed to be crystal-clear about her expectations of him. Or her lack of them. 'Alone?'

She shook her head. She would *die* if he left her alone tonight.

'Not alone, Rashid,' she murmured quietly. 'Together.'

CHAPTER EIGHT

HER heart was pounding as he closed the bedroom door, and she thanked heaven that the room was lit only with the soft light of the lamps. She wanted to see him, but not in too much detail, for she was terrified that she would disappoint him and prove as hopeless a lover as she had done before.

He stood in front of her, surveying her with an unmoving face, the ebony glitter of his eyes and the rapid beat of the pulse at his temple the only outward sign of life.

Her lips parted. 'Rashid,' she breathed threadily, hoping that he would not want more than this to signal her assent. He had told her that he would not beg—well, neither would she!

He saw her raise her chin in defiance and he almost smiled at her gesture of pride. But the moment was far too intense for humour or for battles of will. Because the look in her eyes and the way she had whispered his name told him everything he needed to know.

'Come to me, sweet Jenna,' he commanded softly. 'Come to your Sheikh.'

It was only a few steps, but her legs felt so weak that she feared they would not carry her that short distance. And only the fact that he was standing there, his eyes inviting her into his embrace, ensured that she found herself where she most wanted to be.

She gave a little moan as he pulled her against him, and, catching her face between his hands, bent his head to kiss her in a kiss which was sweet and as potent as strong wine. She felt so dizzy with the sensation of his mouth against her mouth, his tongue flicking an erotic little entry inside, that she barely registered time passing, barely even registered the moment when he slid the zip of her dress down and gently removed it from her body.

The white embroidered dress pooled in a luxurious heap by her feet and she was left in nothing but the extravagant white lace of her lingerie. He made a fierce imprecation beneath his breath as his eyes observed the provocative swell of her breasts, before lifting her into his arms and carrying her across the room like a victor with his trophy, to where the divan awaited them.

'Rashid,' she half protested, but it was a wonderful sensation to be locked in the powerful arms of such a man.

It wasn't until he had lain her down that he looked at her with an expression as close to tenderness as she had ever seen, and her heart came close to melting. Because in that moment she recognised that her love for him burned as strong as it ever had.

'Shall I undress for you now, my sweet Jenna?' he questioned quietly. 'Would you like that?'

The blood thundered in her ears as she nodded, knowing that she would be far too shy to undress him herself. 'Y-yes. Yes, I would.'

With a fluid movement he swept the silken tunic over his head, dropping it carelessly on the floor, enjoying the way the tip of her tongue flicked its way along her lips as his muscular torso was laid bare.

And then he untied the sash of his trousers and heard her tiny gasp as he kicked them away from him.

He saw the startled direction of her eyes, and he looked down at himself and then shrugged. 'You see the effect you have on me, my sweet Jenna?' he mused, but then his voice gentled. 'It will not be as before. I will make you taste pleasure tonight, my sweet desert flower,' he promised softly. 'I will satisfy your each and every need, and when the sun rises in the morning you will have known the rapture and the joy that your beauty and your virtue merits.'

She didn't doubt a word of it, and something in the velvet caress of his voice allayed her fears, so that when he came to join her on the divan she wrapped her arms around him tightly, with greedy possession.

He laughed softly as she pressed her breasts so eagerly

against his hair-roughened chest, and he kissed the top of her head before gently pressing her back against the bed.

'Stay still,' he commanded, and then his eyes glittered with irresistible challenge. 'If you are able.'

She stared at him in confusion, but by then he had taken her bra off, was bending his mouth to her nipple, and she felt such intense pleasure flooding through her as his lips closed around it that she moaned his name aloud.

'Rashid?'

'Shh,' he whispered against the tightened nub, and licked it as luxuriously as he would a lollipop.

And while he suckled her he began taking off her lace panties, very, very slowly, sliding them indolently down over her knees.

'Rashid!' she moaned, for the panties were off and she was as naked as he was, and now he was drifting his fingertips up inside her leg to find the silky flesh of her inner thigh.

'Shh,' he said again, only now his fingertip was no longer on her leg, but touching her very intimately indeed, teasing and moving against the moist skin in a way which was making it impossible for her not to move her hips in a silent yet agonised plea for she knew not what.

'Rashid,' she whispered in mystification. 'What is this?'

He tiptoed the finger with precision against her honeyed flesh and felt her shudder helplessly in response. 'Mmmmm?'

The powerful sensation which was creeping inexorably through her veins made her forget the question she had been asking, and she opened her eyes distractedly to find him watching her. And still he touched her, only now the movement had quickened, and he was bending his head to kiss her…and she felt as though she was going to die…to die or to…

It came upon her with the shock and force of a thunderbolt, her back arching and her legs splaying indolently as wave upon wave of pleasure rocked through her and she moaned against his mouth.

And only when she was completely still did he stop kissing her and raise his head to look down at her, a slow smile lifting his mouth as he saw her look of dreamy contentment, the flush of roses to her cheeks.

She smiled back at him. 'I liked that,' she said shyly.

He laughed with pleasure. 'Yes, I know you did. But that was only the very beginning, my sweet Jenna. There are many, many variations on the act of love, and I intend to explore each and every one with you.'

Just for a moment she felt her heart sink as she thought of all the other women he had known, but ruthlessly she pushed the thought away.

He was her Sheikh and her husband and she was here in his bed—far better to seize the moment and enjoy it than to sadden herself with regrets and hopeless longings for words of love.

He stroked away a damp strand of hair from where it had been glued to her cheek. 'Shall I make you pregnant, Jenna? Would you like that?'

Her heart thudded with disappointment against her ribcage. Was that all part of the deal—a son and heir just as soon as possible? 'W-would you?'

He shook his head. 'Pregnancy changes a woman's whole life. It is not for the man to decide.'

'Well, then—I would like to wait for a while,' she ventured. 'To give ourselves a chance to know one another.'

'Mmmm.' He leaned over and pulled a packet of condoms from a secret drawer in the inlaid locker, then slanted her a lazy smile. 'Starting tonight.'

It wasn't what she had meant, but her doubts were soon forgotten because Rashid had begun to make love to her, and who on earth could think at a time like that?

CHAPTER NINE

'RASHID?'

Rashid paused in the act of tying his sash and looked over at where Jenna lay, her naked body so golden against the snow-white of the sheet. It wasn't easy being married to her—he never wanted to get out of bed in the mornings!

He raised his dark brows quizzically. 'Yes, my sweet?'

She squinted at her watch. 'You are up very early. Are you...are you going away?' She nearly said *again*, but she bit the vulnerable word back.

He nodded his gleaming dark head and glanced at the time. 'I am afraid so, Jenna. I must travel to the eastern region with haste.'

'Why?'

His eyes narrowed. 'Oh, nothing that need concern you, my sweet.'

No, of course not. Politics was not the business of a wife. It was always the same. Her heart lurched. 'And will you be away for long, my Sheikh?'

'For as long as it takes, Jenna—no longer.'

She could tell from his voice that the subject was closed and she must be satisfied with his rather curt explanation—except that satisfied she most certainly wasn't. No way. Except in the purely physical sense, of course—Rashid seemed able to fulfil her every wish and her every desire, and invent a whole lot more into the bargain.

But ever since they had returned from their honeymoon she had discovered for herself just what was expected of the wife of the Sheikh—how she herself was nothing more than an isolated figurehead. And how their two worlds barely touched.

She had her charity work and he had his affairs of state—

a demanding and taxing role as Ruler which took him away from her far more than she would have dreamed of.

So much for putting off having a baby so that she could get to know him—why, she barely saw him! The closeness which had been reawoken between them during those two glorious weeks of their honeymoon seemed to have vanished into nothing once they returned to the busy life of the palace.

Everyone wanted him. His advisors wanted him. His politicians wanted him. Foreign countries wanted him. She wanted him, too—but the only time he was ever completely hers was in their marital bed, when he took her to paradise and back again without fail.

But even that seemed strangely empty once the pleasures of fulfilment had receded and he had fallen into an exhausted sleep by her side. The words of love she longed to tell him remained unsaid—for Rashid was a man who seemed to have no time for terms of endearment. He told her that she was beautiful, yes, and he told her that her body pleased him greatly—but the lavish compliments only served to emphasise that she did not have what she most desired.

His heart.

'Can't I come with you, Rashid?' she asked plaintively. 'Just this once?'

He frowned. 'That will not be possible. You have your committees, Jenna, and I am told that your contribution to them is invaluable. Do you not wish to serve your country, my sweet?'

She heard the unmistakable disapproval in his voice and suppressed the sigh which would anger him further. She was not his partner. Nor his equal. Only when she had accepted that would she ever be able to find the inner peace she yearned for.

'Then at least come and kiss me goodbye,' she murmured.

He did as she asked, feeling the sharp tug of desire as he bent his lips to the softness of hers and then ran his fingers through her hair. 'It is almost down to your shoulders now,' he murmured. 'Much better.'

'Thank you. I am glad that my Sheikh approves,' she said

demurely, and sat up, and saw his eyes darken as her bare breasts were revealed.

'Do you know how much you tempt me?' He sighed regretfully. 'All my officials are waiting for me, but how I wish I could lose myself in you.' He moved away from the bed before he was lost in the weakness of that temptation.

With an aching heart she watched him leave and then lay back down on the divan again, staring sightlessly up at the high ceiling above her.

It was not as she had hoped it would be—in fact it was a million miles away from how she had hoped it would be. He didn't *talk* to her. Or confide in her. Or ask her advice. In six months of marriage he had seemed preoccupied the whole time, and Jenna felt like just a tiny, tiny fragment of his life. Yet deep down she had known and feared that it was going to be like this, for was it not the royal custom? Separate lives. His father had had a marriage which had been very similar, and his father before him—everyone in Quador knew that.

Her own parents' marriage had been exceptionally close, but that had been a rarity. High-born Quadorian men usually took mistresses. She knew that, and yet it did not stop her from yearning for that same kind of closeness with Rashid—a closeness he did not seem remotely interested in giving her.

He was gone for five long days, with two crackled and annoyingly brief telephone calls their only communication.

And then the very thing she had been most dreading happened.

She was just emerging from a committee she had been chairing which had discussed setting up a hostel for battered wives, when one of her ladies-in-waiting gave her a message from Rashid.

It was stark and to the point.

I have to fly straight to Paris on urgent business and will probably be away for the week. I will ring you the moment I get the opportunity.

Paris?

Paris? Where Chantal lived and no doubt waited for the dark Sheikh.

Her face blanched and she crumpled the paper with a whitened knuckle.

'It is bad news, mistress?' asked the lady-in-waiting anxiously.

The very worst. Rashid had been given the perfect excuse to meet up with his mistress. Unless that was the real purpose behind his visit—and she had no way of finding out for Abdullah would tell her nothing. She shook her head. 'No, it's nothing,' she lied painfully. 'I will be—I will be in my office should there be any call from the Sheikh.'

In her office she paced up and down and her heart pounded with fear and jealousy. It was only what she had expected, and yet the actuality was a million times more disturbing than her fevered imaginings.

He was a man of relentless sexual appetite with a taste for the exotic. And he was used to variety. His stream of lovers had been legendary—so why on earth should that have changed? His father had taken mistresses—it had been an open secret at court. Six months of marriage had probably left Rashid feeling jaded and bored, no matter how much she tried to please him.

Her hand trembled. She couldn't share him! She would *not* share him! She would sooner be without him than be able to bear the thought of him in another woman's arms!

Her fingers still shaking, she picked up the telephone and rang her sister on the other side of the world. 'Nadia?'

'Jenna, is that you?'

'Of course it's me.'

'But you sound *terrible*—what on earth is the matter?'

'R-Rashid has flown to Paris.'

'And?'

'Nadia—he has a mistress in Paris.'

'*Had* a mistress,' Nadia corrected gently. 'He's married to you now, remember?'

As if she could forget! 'I have to know if he's seeing her, Nadia,' she said urgently. 'I can't live my life like this—I *have* to find out!'

'Well, can't you just fly to Paris and surprise him?'

Jenna shook her head. 'Oh, sure—he's surrounded by minders and aides who would lie through their teeth for him! If I announced that I was taking a plane to Paris he would probably hear about it before the airline did!' An idea began to take root in her mind. 'Unless I was arranging to meet *you* for a holiday in London, of course!'

'London isn't Paris,' Nadia pointed out.

'I know it isn't—but I could catch a train from London straight to Paris.'

'And what about your bodyguards? Can you really see *them* letting you do that?'

Jenna gave a small tight smile at her strained reflection. 'You know how people always say how similar we look?' she queried softly. 'Why, if you were wearing my clothes and I was wearing yours—well, anyone could easily mistake us for one another!'

'Jenna—you aren't suggesting what I think you're suggesting, are you? Are you going to pretend to be *me*?'

'How long have I covered up for you and Brad?'

'That's blackmail,' her sister objected jokingly.

'Or you could say that one good turn deserves another.' There was a pause. 'So how soon can you fly to London?' Jenna asked crisply.

Her plans proved almost ridiculously easy to execute. She arrived in London accompanied by a lady-in-waiting and two bodyguards and went straight to the large penthouse suite at the Granchester hotel, which Nadia had booked.

She hadn't seen her sister since the wedding, and the two of them embraced tearfully.

'Jenna, what on earth are you going to *say* to Rashid?' asked Nadia worriedly. 'Won't he go mad if he finds out you've been checking up on him? And won't someone tell him that you've left Quador?'

'I don't care. I have to find out the truth,' said Jenna urgently. 'The man I married is like a stranger to me.'

'Already?' asked Nadia sadly.

'Except during our honeymoon, when we seemed as close as a couple could be.'

'But you love him? You do still love him, don't you?'

'As life itself,' answered Jenna simply. 'That much has not changed. But I can't live a lie, Nadia—and my love for him will be eaten away if he intends to be free with other women. I would sooner divorce him than have that happen.'

'He would never allow it, Jenna—you know that.'

'We shall see. We're in the twenty-first century now, not the Dark Ages—he cannot keep me a prisoner to his will!'

Jenna sent one of the bodyguards out with her lady-in-waiting to pick up a coat she had ordered from one of London's most exclusive department stores and then she dressed in some of Nadia's unashamedly American clothes.

And by nine o'clock that evening she found herself safely alone in Paris, speeding along in a taxi towards the Splendide, where Rashid always stayed when he was in the city.

Unless he was at Chantal's, she thought, with a painful lurch of her heart.

She went straight up to his suite and the door was opened by Abdullah, his look of confusion quickly becoming one of wariness as he registered just who it was standing there, in blue jeans and a black leather jacket.

'Mistress,' he said slowly, and bowed his head.

'I have come to see the Sheikh.'

There was a pause. 'The Sheikh is not expecting you.'

It was unmistakably a reprimand, but Jenna forced a smile onto lips which felt as though they had been carved from ice. 'I want to surprise him.'

'The Sheikh is not here, mistress.'

'And I suppose you're not going to tell me where he is, Abdullah?'

'You know that I cannot do that, mistress.'

Her skin prickled and her smile faded as she marched past him. 'Then I shall wait.'

She didn't have to wait long. She had only been slumped in an armchair for less than ten minutes, watching a French soap opera in a vain attempt to try to keep her heart-rending thoughts at bay, when Rashid entered the luxury suite.

She heard him before she saw him. Heard the urgent words spoken to him in an undertone by Abdullah. And then suddenly he was there, filling the room with his magnificent and rather daunting presence. She searched his impassive face for any tell-tale signs of betrayal. Where had he been? Had his naked limbs been entwined with Chantal's? Where had he *been*?

He stood looking at her, his face as dark and as unforgiving as thunder, but she was too angry to care.

'Would you care to explain the meaning of this unwarranted intrusion?' he hissed.

Intrusion! 'And would you care to explain just where you have been until this hour?' she retorted furiously.

'I'll tell you where I have been, you little fool—I have been at the British Embassy in an attempt to find out your whereabouts!' he stormed. 'I have had half the police force in London scouring the city. And your sister—who I gather you were supposed to be meeting—is nowhere to be found either! What the hell are you doing *here*, Jenna? And where the *hell* are your bodyguards?'

'I gave them the slip!' she boasted, blithely ignoring the look of dark menace on his face. 'I dressed as Nadia and took the shuttle from London!'

'You did *what*?'

'You heard!'

He was almost beside himself with fury as he strode over to confront her, and he very nearly hauled her angrily into his arms—until he reminded himself what would happen if he did *that*. 'You fool,' he grated again. 'Didn't you stop to think about the danger you were placing yourself in?'

'I can take care of myself, Rashid! I did without bodyguards for most of my life and I can function perfectly well without them!'

'Not as my *wife*, you can't!'

'Oh, your wife!' she scorned. 'What's in a name? What kind of a *wife* am I, Rashid? And, more importantly, what kind of a husband are you?'

He went very still. 'And just what is that supposed to mean?'

'Think about it!' she stormed, but at least she felt alive again. At least the tiptoeing around his feelings and trying to guess at his needs had been replaced by a vivid but liberating *honesty*. 'What have you been doing since you've been in Paris?'

The black eyes glittered dangerously. 'What do *you* think I've been doing, Jenna?'

The bitter words came tumbling out before she could stop them. 'Making love to your mistress, I expect! *Chantal*! I expect it's nearly *killed* you to be faithful to me for six long months, hasn't it, Rashid? Assuming, of course, that you *have* been faithful?'

His dark skin paled. 'How *dare* you speak to me this way?'

'But I'm your wife now, Rashid! Aren't I entitled to my opinions—?'

'Not if they are a complete fabrication!' he snapped.

'Well, how about a few answers, then?'

He controlled his breathing with difficulty. 'You really think that I've spent the evening making love to Chantal?' he questioned incredulously.

'Don't ever speak her name in front of me!' She shot him a blistering look, conveniently forgetting that *she* had been the one to bring the woman's name up. 'Were you?'

'Of course I was not. I told you—I've been at the damned embassy!'

'There's no ''of course'' about it, Rashid. You haven't spent the last two days at the embassy, have you? What else am I to think? You could easily have made love to her! And don't try to tell me that she wouldn't still want you to—because what woman wouldn't?'

He very nearly thanked her for the compliment, but resisted. He had never seen her in such a rage! 'But *you* are the woman I make love to. *You* are my wife, Jenna,' he stated softly.

'Except that I'm not—not really. Am I?' she finished in a small, broken question.

He saw all the fight and the anger leave her, to be replaced by a sadness which smote him like a blow from a sword. 'You want the truth?' he questioned huskily.

She shook her head. 'I *don't know*!'

'Well, whether you want it or not—you *need* to know it, Jenna.'

'Rashid—'

'The day after I asked you to marry me, yes, I *did* come to Paris—'

'Don't!' She shuddered, but he did not heed her plea.

'I told Chantal that it was over, that you were to be my bride and yes, she wanted me to make love to her—'

'Oh, *don't*!' she begged again, but he shook his dark head resolutely.

'I told her no,' he continued inexorably. 'I have not spoken to her since and I have no intention of doing so.'

Her eyes opened very wide. 'Really?'

'Really.' His voice softened. 'Jenna, what makes you think that I would betray you? Do you think that the vows I made on our wedding day were meaningless?'

She shook her head. 'How do I know *what* you would do,' she asked in frustration, 'when you won't let me near you?'

He frowned. 'But we share a room each night—'

'When you're *there*!' she argued. 'And I'm not talking about physically, anyway, Rashid—I'm talking about emotionally!'

'Emotionally?' he echoed, as if he was unfamiliar with the word.

'Yes, emotionally,' she said tiredly. 'Apart from on our honeymoon, I feel as though I might as well be living with a robot!'

'You have many, many insults for me this evening, don't you, Jenna?' he observed quietly.

'I don't mean to insult you—I'm just telling you how I feel. And don't glower at me like that, Rashid! I know you've had a lifetime of people revering you and only ever speaking to you when you initiate the conversation! But what is the point of being married if we aren't going to be close to one another?'

The black eyes glittered. 'You have complaints about our marriage, Jenna?'

'Yes, I do!' She drew a deep breath, knowing that she might never have another chance to say this. 'You never *talk* to me, do you? You never tell me about your day! Half the time you won't say where you're going, or what you're doing—or who with—so of course my imagination works overtime! And you never seem to stop working, either! When was the last time we spent some quality time together that wasn't in bed? I'll tell you when—on our honeymoon, and that was six months ago!'

He stared at her with eyes which were filled with a sudden, dawning comprehension. 'I once told you that I had a problem with delegation,' he mused slowly. 'And now it seems that this is a skill which I must embrace more wholeheartedly.' He sighed. 'No, I do not confide affairs of state to you, it is true,' he agreed. 'But do you not know that knowledge can be a dangerous weapon, Jenna? That if you were aware of all the ramifications of what goes on in Quador I would be putting you at risk?'

'How?'

His black eyes were very sombre. 'Do you not know, my sweet, that there are still factions in the country who would wish to overthrow your Sheikh? When you asked if you could accompany me to the Eastern region the other day, I said no. I didn't say why—that there were very real dangers at play at that time.'

'Then why didn't you just *tell* me that?'

'Would you not have worried about me?'

'Of course I would!'

'Well, then.'

'It isn't just about the not confiding, Rashid—you never...'

She had her pride, but pride itself could be dangerous if it prevented you from discovering the truth, and she had to know. She *had* to.

'I never what?' he prompted softly, for her mouth had taken on a tremulous shape that made him want to kiss it.

'You never tell me how you feel.'

'About what?'

'About *me*!' she burst out. 'You never tell me that you love me, which can only lead me to assume that you don't! And if you don't love me, then it's obvious that you will stray eventually.'

His mouth hardened. 'What right do I have to speak of love to you?' he questioned bitterly. 'When I took your innocence so brutally and then forced you into marrying me?'

'You didn't rape me, Rashid,' she pointed out.

'But I might as well have done!' he raged. 'I showed no restraint! No control! I have never behaved like that in my life before!'

'And neither have I! We both got carried away in the heat of the moment—it wasn't anybody's *fault*!'

'But *I* was the experienced one,' he asserted harshly. 'I should have stopped in time. And I couldn't,' he finished harshly. 'I just couldn't.'

'So what? Is it such a major crime that just for once in your life you failed to live up to your own exacting standards?' she demanded. 'If you really want to know—I feel quite powerful that I should have been the one to make you lose control like that. If it's forgiveness you want, then I've forgiven you, Rashid—if only you could forgive yourself.'

He stared at her for a long moment. 'But I still forced you to marry me, didn't I, Jenna?' he said slowly. 'When the idea was clearly so abhorrent to you.'

'And don't you know why?'

He shook his head. 'Because your feelings for me had died?'

'They never died, Rashid,' she said, and a small, rueful smile broke through. 'Even though I tried like anything to kill them off.'

He reached out a fingertip and smoothed it down the smooth surface of her cheek. 'And why would you do that?'

'Because I kept reading about all your lovers in the newspapers,' she admitted brokenly. 'And I was as jealous as hell of them.'

He gave up trying to keep her at arm's length and pulled her into his arms, staring deep into her amber eyes. All along he had tried to protect her, but he saw now that by doing so he had only succeeded in making her insecure.

'There have been lovers, yes,' he said quietly, and he saw her flinch. 'But not nearly so many as the newspapers reported.'

She flinched. One would be too many! 'Why any?' she whispered. 'Why not just me?'

He shook his head and tried to explain. 'Jenna, my father's marriage was not one I intended to replicate—but I am a pragmatist, and a realist. I knew that when I married you I intended to be utterly faithful, but I was unable to offer you my fidelity until then. We couldn't marry before you left—I had only recently come into the Sheikhdom, and I needed to give myself wholeheartedly to my country.'

He stared at her, and his voice grew quiet and serious. 'I needed to live a little, to experience something of the world—to give in to some of the temptations of the flesh so that those temptations would not haunt me for the rest of my life. Does that sound incredibly selfish?'

She thought about it. 'Yes, I suppose it does,' she said honestly. Jenna had a pragmatic streak herself, and she was now beginning to see why Rashid had acted as he had. She might not like it, but she could understand it. Not that she was going to let him know that. Not yet. 'Particularly as you would have gone berserk if I had done the same thing.'

'This much is true,' he admitted, and his eyes were rueful as he touched the tips of her fingers to his lips. 'You think it unfair?' he questioned.

'I don't *think* it's unfair, I *know* it's unfair!' she retorted, knowing in her heart that it had not seemed that way to her.

But then, she had never really wanted any other man in the way that she wanted her Sheikh.

He nodded. 'Yes. As in so much of life, sweet Jenna mine.' He looked down into her upturned face and saw the question in her beautiful eyes.

Say it, she thought, unable to look away from his glittering ebony gaze. Please just say it. Tell me that all these years I haven't cherished false hopes. Tell me what I felt on our honeymoon was real. Even if it is incomplete, tell me that there is something between us which could grow and grow.

'I love you, Jenna,' he said simply, but she heard the unfamiliar tremble of emotion in his voice.

Tears brightened her eyes and then his voice became urgent. 'Don't you know that, my own sweet love? Believe me when I tell you that I have always loved you. *Always*,' he breathed, but his face tightened with a fleeting look of regret. 'I thought I needed to find out what I was missing,' he sighed. 'Only now I realise that I wasn't missing anything at all.'

'But you let me go away to America,' she accused, though as accusations went it was pretty much on the gentle side.

'Don't you know why?' he demanded. 'I had just inherited a country in turmoil—so how in heaven's name could I have taken on a wife at the same time?'

'And if I'd stayed then you couldn't have gone on having all your other women, could you?' she asked jealously.

'If you'd stayed I would have been unable to think or eat or sleep or breathe with the frustration of wanting you,' he admitted heatedly. 'Your beauty exploded into life like a flower, my sweet Jenna, and it so captured me with its sweet perfume that I was unable to think of anything else. And certainly not about Quador.' He bent his face close to hers. 'Oh, Jenna—can you still find it in your heart to love me, my wife?'

For the first time in her life she saw vulnerability written on the proud, cold face of a man whom she had always considered to be invulnerable.

But beneath the magnificent body and the heavy weight of his destiny he was reaching out for her in a way she had always dreamed of. Stripping away the proud and arrogant exterior to show her, and only her, the heart of the man which lay beneath.

'Can you?' he repeated huskily. 'Love me?'

She felt filled with a new and heady kind of power, and she curved her lips into a thoughtful smile.

'I can,' she agreed serenely.

He briefly closed his eyes and expelled a long, shuddering breath, unaware that he had been holding it. 'And I will spend the rest of my life showing you how much I love you,' he promised shakily.

It was time to test out her new power! 'I shall look forward to that,' she purred, but shook her head as he lowered his mouth to claim hers in a kiss. 'On two conditions, Rashid.'

'Conditions?' He frowned the frown of a man who was unused to making concessions of any kind. 'What kind of conditions?' he asked suspiciously. 'And how many?'

'Only two,' she answered demurely.

'Then name them!'

'Firstly, I want to use my law training to help negotiate the freedom of the Quador press.'

'A free press?' Rashid demanded. 'It is unheard of!'

'In the past, yes. But the internet has made news so accessible,' she argued. 'You know it has! So why must we be dragged kicking and screaming into the twenty-first century, my love? Why not embrace change willingly?'

He frowned, unable to fault her logic. 'And the second condition?' he growled.

'I want you to persuade my father to allow my sister to marry the man she loves.'

CHAPTER TEN

THE band was playing as Rashid smiled down into his wife's eyes. 'A very different wedding from our own,' he observed softly.

She smiled back at him. These days she never seemed to stop smiling! 'Outwardly, very different indeed,' she agreed, her voice low. 'But you were the one who once told me that a wedding is a wedding is a wedding. And the emotion is the same for everyone, surely?'

He shook his head. 'No man could love a woman as much as I love you, Jenna,' he declared.

Well, she certainly wasn't going to argue with *that*!

They were gathered at one of Long Island's most glittering hotels, waiting for the wedding of her sister Nadia to Brad Toulmin, a ceremony made possible by the intervention of her Sheikh.

Jenna had told Rashid all about Nadia and Brad's forbidden love affair, and his calm and accepting reaction had both surprised and delighted her.

'The ways of the heart are mysterious,' he had commented thoughtfully. 'What use will it serve if they are forced to part and Nadia comes home to marry a Quadorian if she is not happy? No use at all!' he had finished passionately.

It had been Rashid himself who had broken the news to her father.

'Two such different cultures!' her father had protested. 'It is rare for such a union to last!'

'But you married an American yourself, Bulent,' Rashid had pointed out softly. 'Why should your daughter not do the same?'

It was unarguable logic and the older man had caved in immediately.

And of course, as Jenna had gleefully told Nadia afterwards, how could their father possibly refuse Rashid anything? He *was* the Sheikh!

The wedding was to be held in the extravagant flower-laden gardens of the hotel, and Jenna was brimming over with excitement. And with love. It seemed scarcely credible that it was over a year since their own wedding. The last six months had whizzed by like six seconds, and they had been so very happy together. She looked up to find her husband watching her closely.

'What is it?' she questioned.

He smiled. Sometimes he felt as though she could read his mind! Come to think of it, she probably could! She could certainly twist him with great ease around her little finger. He had made many concessions to his fiery wife to improve the quality of their life together—and had actually discovered that he enjoyed making them, much to his surprise. He had begun to delegate more, and to trust her with his confidences. And every week they spent a whole day and night together which were set aside just for the two of them.

But Jenna was busy herself these days, helping to free the Quador Press—to the complete astonishment of the world at large.

'You know that such a move will boost your international standing, Rashid,' she had told her husband winningly.

And of course she had been right.

He sighed with a tender indulgence. When was she ever wrong?

'Do you grow more beautiful with each day that passes?' he questioned softly, thinking how radiant she looked today.

'Well, I certainly hope so,' she said demurely, and then looked up at him. 'Do you still want to give me a baby, darling?'

He nodded and traced the outline of her lip with the tip of his finger. 'Yes, I do—but I'm not sure that I can bear to share you with anyone just yet,' he admitted slowly. 'Imagine what my people would say if they knew that!'

She hid a smile. The Rashid of old would never have put

his feelings on the line like that! But she had taught him that communication was vital in a happy marriage. And that love and showing your feelings never equalled weakness. 'Then we'll wait a little longer, shall we?'

'You don't mind?'

She shook her head. 'The only thing I would ever mind would be if I didn't have you,' she said seriously.

'Then only death shall part us, my sweet.' And he brushed his lips against hers, feeling her shiver beneath him, loving her instant responsiveness. 'I wish I could take you to bed right now,' he said huskily.

The band began to strike up the 'Wedding March', and Jenna slipped her hand into his.

'You'll have to wait for that too, my Sheikh.'

'Not for too long,' he growled, sizzling her a look of hungry intent which set her heart racing.

'N-no, not for too long,' she agreed unsteadily, and with a harmony of body language which reflected their closeness more than words ever could they both turned round to watch the marriage service begin.

Kate Walker

THE DUKE'S SECRET WIFE

CHAPTER ONE

So SHE was here at last.

Luis de Silva watched from the shadows as the small group strolled towards him. There were perhaps twelve or fifteen of them, of assorted ages and nationalities. About them there was the buzz of faint excitement and anticipation, and they were clearly oblivious to the chill of the early spring evening.

But it was the young woman in the middle of the group who caught and held Luis's attention.

'Isabella…'

The name hissed through his teeth on the instinctive indrawn breath he couldn't control.

It was two years since he had seen her but he would have recognised her anywhere. There was no mistaking the sleek, shining cap of blonde hair that gleamed silver in the moonlight. Her tall, slender figure was clothed in a dark velvet dress; green, he suspected, though the gathering shadows of evening made it impossible to tell for sure. Full length, and mediaeval in style, it had wide, silk-lined sleeves, falling almost to the ground from her fine-boned wrists. It was cinched around her slim waist with an ornate gold belt, and over the top she wore a heavy black cloak that swirled around her with every graceful movement.

'Madre de Dios!'

Luis choked back the exclamation that rose to his lips, taking several hasty steps backwards into the shadows of the nearby buildings. He did not want to be seen until he was ready. It would mean losing the element of surprise he was determined would be on his side when he finally revealed himself to her.

But for now he was content to watch.

'And so, ladies and gentlemen, we come to the site of one of the darkest events in the whole of the history of York…'

Her voice was light and sweet-toned; her actor's training meant that it carried clearly across to where he stood watching her.

'This building is Clifford's Tower…'

The words blurred and scrambled inside his head, making no sense. Instead, he was swept away on a tide of memory he neither wanted nor welcomed as just the sound of that once well-known voice opened up the door to the part of his past he would sooner forget.

Once that voice had made his heart lift so high he had thought it might actually escape his body. It had made his senses kick on a pulse of desire so hot and strong that he had been totally at their mercy.

But most of all, it had once spoken to him of love and trust and belief in another until he had forgotten all his natural caution and fallen head over heels into the first, the most powerful, the only love of his life.

But then she had taken that love and crushed it underneath the heel of one of her elegantly shod feet. And now…

'No!'

Furious with himself, he refused to let his thoughts wander any further. He would not let himself think of those times. Could not let himself remember or he would turn and walk away from here, never looking back.

And he couldn't afford to look back.

In the background a church clock chimed the half-hour, reminding Luis that the young man, a student he presumed, he had bribed to let him take his place had said that it was around now he should hear his cue. What was it he had said?

'But before we move on…'

He'd waited long enough. He was going to have to do this so it was better to get it over with.

The muscles in his jaw tightened, his shoulders tensed, and he stepped out into the light of the street lamp.

'Isabella…'

It was the last thing Isabelle had anticipated. With her mind firmly fixed on following her script, determined to get her timing exactly right, she had been oblivious to everything else around her. This group of tourists who had followed her around the carefully planned route of the York City Ghost Walk had clearly enjoyed every minute of it. Their enthusiasm bubbled in the air, sparking off her invention so that she had ad-libbed outrageously. And now they were approaching the climax of the night.

But first there was one more 'apparition' to tantalise them. Any minute now, when she spoke his cue, Andy would appear from the darkness, dressed as Dick Turpin, the famous highwayman, and say...

'Isabella...'

The voice came from behind her, from where she had expected that Andy would appear. But it was not Andy. The voice was nothing like Andy's Yorkshire tones for one, and...

Isabella.

Only one man had ever called her that. Had ever added the extra syllable to her name. To make it easier, he had always claimed, for his Spanish tongue.

Only one man had pronounced the four syllables in quite that lilting way, turning her name into a form of poetry that twisted in her heart with the bitterness of memory.

Only one man had ever spoken to her with quite that accent. But this could not be him. That man had left her life two years before, vowing never, ever to return. He was thousands of miles away, in another country, another world.

He could *not* be here!

'Buenas tardes, mi mujer,' that taunting, terrifyingly familiar voice continued, pushing her into whirling round, eyes wide, fearful of who she might see.

'Luis!'

It was a choking cry of stunned disbelief and horror as she took in the lean, powerful height of him, the forceful width of chest and shoulders, under the black jacket and jeans, the dark, glossy hair and brilliant, gleaming eyes, and she took a couple of hasty steps backwards in an instinctive urge to flight.

'L-Luis? Is that you?'

The tall, dark man took another couple of steps forward, moving right into the pool of light shed by a street lamp. And Isabelle knew with a terrible sense of inevitability that there was no chance of escape. No hope that she had made a mistake.

The two years since she had seen him had changed him little. He had matured in that time, obviously, and now, at thirty, he was a man in his prime. He had filled out, any lingering awkwardness of youth being replaced by powerful muscles and a dignified control that gave every movement an elegant restraint, like the approach of a prowling hunting cat.

'Good evening, *querida*.'

The rich, deep voice seemed to curl around her senses like warm smoke, making her nerves prickle just under the delicate surface of her skin. With her ears accustomed to the flat vowels of the Yorkshire accent, his intonation seemed even more exotic and foreign than ever, making her feel as if some alien and dangerous visitor had just intruded into her happy and secure way of life.

'What a pleasure it is to see you again,' he drawled, his smile a flicker of pure menace, teeth very white against the tanned skin of his face.

'Now that I really doubt!'

Isabelle was gradually regaining some degree of control over her reactions. Okay, so her heart was pounding in double-quick time, her breath coming in a distinctly uneven pattern, but she was determined not to let him see that.

'I don't think that *pleasure* would be the right word.'

'Well, then, you would be wrong, *mi angel*,' Luis drawled in a voice as smooth as silk. 'You would be completely wrong.'

As he spoke he let his darkened gaze drift downwards, over the shock-whitened skin of her cheeks, past the fine lines of her throat, to the creamy flesh of her breasts exposed by the low-cut neckline of her velvet gown. The slight curves were pushed upwards and forwards by the tight lacing and the bones in the bodice, so that they were enhanced and displayed in a

way sh
itively u

'Pleas

'For y

Instinct

enveloping

the sudden

with a ting

made matter

only embarra

In spite of

push down the

citement, a bet

This man had a

she had hoped t

the impact of that

then she was bitte

'I had hoped that you'd meant it—that

'I had hoped.'

away for good.'

'That was my original intention

And I have had to change means

'And this change means

'That we have going to

'He was going to

The words so

hopes she mi

relationshi

all the

...uduced

...tual good looks,

If anything, the ..... was even stronger because she hadn't seen him in so long.

'I thought that you never, ever wanted to see me again. At least, that was what you said the last time I saw you.'

The time that he had flung his wedding ring in her face and told her that the shop they had bought it from might actually take it back.

'If you're lucky,' he had spat at her, his bitterly scathing tone seeming to flay several layers of skin from her vulnerable body, 'you might even get a full refund. After all, it hasn't been on my finger long enough to show any wear and tear. Barely long enough to consummate our union—but that was quite long enough for you to grow tired and bored and look for new amusements.'

Then she had been too stunned, too devastated, to fight him. She hadn't been able to find the words to convince him he was wrong and to call him back. Now all the pain, the horror of that moment came flooding back, putting a biting bitterness into her tone as she faced him with what she hoped looked like confidence.

you planned to stay

But circumstances change.
them.'

precisely what?'

to discuss. Your letter, for one.'

gree to a divorce.

nded in her head like the death knell to any

nt have had that one day they could revive their

p. That somehow they could find a way to get past

hurt, the lies and devastation on both sides, and find a

y to get through to each other again.

They had been so in love once. And deep down inside she knew that she had never truly given up on the hope that that love wasn't totally dead. That there was still a chance it could live again.

But Luis's expression had nothing of love in it. It was hard and cold, the eyes that she knew to be a glittering golden brown were shuttered and withdrawn from her, hooded by heavy lids with thick, black, lustrously curling lashes. And it had been because she had known that this was how he would react that she had finally made that act of desperation and written asking for a divorce.

'We can talk here.'

'Not in front of an audience.'

The autocratic gesture he made brought her attention back to the fact that they were not alone. Stunned and confused, Isabelle belatedly remembered the Ghost Walk group who still stood clustered about them, their original smiles of approval and appreciation changing by turn to frowns of confusion and then to concern. Clearly this was no longer part of the Ghost Walk performance. And, equally obviously, their guide was genuinely distressed.

Now one of the Americans moved forwards.

'Are you all right, miss? Is this guy bothering you?'

'He…'

Luis turned to face him, proud head held arrogantly high,

all his breeding and status showing in every haughty line of his body.

'This *guy*...' he echoed, injecting a biting satire into the words. 'Allow me to introduce myself. I am Don Luis Alejandro de Silva, heir to the Dukedom of Madrigalo.'

He waited a nicely calculated moment for the impact of the title and the innate, bone-deep pride that went with it to hit home on the other man, then coolly and cold-bloodedly went for the knockout verbal punch.

'I also happen to be the lady's husband.'

That caused a ripple of shock to flow through the group, murmurs of astonishment and confusion greeting the announcement.

'Is this true, ma'am?'

For one brief, weak-kneed moment, Isabelle actually considered saying no, this man was not her husband. He was nothing to her; never had been anything in her life. But almost immediately she reconsidered.

For one thing, she dreaded the thought of the possible consequences. Luis de Silva in this sort of coldly determined mood was imposing enough, but Luis angry was quite another matter. And he would be angry—furious—if she denied her relationship with him. He might have rejected that relationship, declared he wanted nothing more to do with her, but he wasn't going to stand by and let her do the same.

'Yes,' she said tiredly, her voice a flat monotone. 'Yes, Don Luis is my husband. It's just that I wasn't expecting to see him. We—we've been separated for some years.'

'So naturally my appearance was something of a shock to her.'

Luis's tone made Isabelle blink hard in bewilderment. In a split second he had switched from being pure blue-blooded aristocrat, arrogant and condescending as could be, and adopted a softer, more affable mood, using a matey, all men together approach.

And the new technique was working. She could see it in the faces of the group around her. The women were quite simply melting in the warmth of that deliberate charm, the carefully switched-on smile, the lowered, deeper voice. And the men were nodding understanding. Even the American, her self-appointed protector, was clearly having second thoughts.

'But, believe me, I mean her no harm. I simply want to talk to her. I had to resort to this subterfuge simply in order to get her attention. I've been trying to get in touch with her for days but she doesn't answer the door—her phone is never picked up.'

'I've been away!' Isabelle interjected, but she might as well not have spoken.

Luis had the group in the palm of his hand. His act was near perfect, giving the impression of being a concerned husband who only wanted to mend the rift that had arisen between himself and his wife. A rift that had been something and nothing, his attitude implied.

And they were swallowing it. Every word.

'I could not wait any longer...'

He didn't need that faintly wry shrug of his powerful shoulders, the supremely Spanish gesture with his hands, Isabelle thought cynically. But he used them anyway. They were his trump card, saying without words that he couldn't help himself. That he was only a man, and a passionate man at that. A man who was so in love with his wife that he couldn't endure another moment's separation from her.

All around her, the murmured comments told Isabelle that Luis had won. He had swung the group's loyalty to his side and there was no way she could fight that.

'I really needed some time alone with her. I'm sure you understand.'

Oh, yes, they understood all right. But at least the chivalrous American wanted to be sure.

'Will you be okay?' he asked solicitously.

'Oh, yes, I'll be fine,' Isabelle assured him emphatically. 'Really I will.'

It was nothing less than the truth. Whatever his faults—and he had plenty of them—Luis was not a thug. He was hot-tempered, ruthless, totally convinced of his supremacy above all others, arrogant as the devil, but he would never knowingly hurt her.

At least not physically.

Emotionally it was a very different matter. That way he could hurt her simply by existing. By existing and not loving her as much as she had loved him. And when that 'not loving' had turned to hate, that was when he had totally devastated her soul.

But she wasn't prepared to give in to him so easily. If you let him, Luis was perfectly capable of riding roughshod over anyone else's feelings.

'But I can't come with you now, Luis. I'm at work—this is my job. I have this tour to finish.'

'I am aware of that, *mi angel*.'

If she had hoped to disconcert him, then clearly it hadn't worked.

'And that is why I have made arrangements...'

One long, bronzed hand was lifted in an autocratic gesture, summoning someone from the darkness of a shop front.

'Señor Morris!'

Isabelle's heart sank to somewhere on the pavement, beneath the soles of her neat ankle boots, as, in answer to the command, the errant Andy, resplendent in his highwayman costume, appeared out of the shadows and strolled towards them, a slightly sheepish grin on his boyish face.

'I'll take over for you, Izzy,' he said. 'I know the rest of the route from here—and all the stories.'

'But...'

She tried to protest but her weak-voiced interjection was ignored as Luis took things right out of her hands.

'*Señoras y señores*, thank you for your patience with this unexpected interruption to your evening. I trust you realise that I would never have acted in this way if I had not thought it was the only thing I could do. Andrew here will be your guide from now on. If you will follow him...'

And they did. Isabelle could only stand and watch as the group headed off, with Andy launching straight into the familiar patter about the history of Clifford's Tower. What else could she possibly do? Luis had outmanoeuvred her, check-mated her like a chess Grand Master.

Not that she was going to give in without a fight.

'So now they've gone…'

Whirling, she faced Luis, her chin coming up defiantly, her eyes flashing challengingly.

'What exactly did you want to talk to me about?'

'Not here.' He shook his dark head.

'Yes! Here and now!'

If he was going to tell her that he agreed to a divorce, then she wanted it over and done with. Wanted the words spoken, the blow delivered. It was like waiting to hear that some part of her had to be amputated. Better to get it done, quickly and sharply. Hopefully, the event would hurt less that way. It was the pain that was waiting for her in the future that she couldn't bear to think about.

'Say what you have to say, Luis…'

'I said not here! I do not want the whole world knowing my business.'

He couldn't just blurt this out cold, here in the street. If he did, he was sure she would just laugh in his face and walk away.

'My car is parked just here. We will go back to your house.'

'We will do no such thing!'

Each minute she spent with him was only making things so much worse. Making it harder to let him go a second time. After those long, lonely years without him, just the sight of him was like a banquet to someone dying of starvation. She couldn't look at him enough, couldn't take enough of him in to appease her hungry senses.

And if she ever let him into her home, then it would be much worse. She would never be able to forget that he had been there; never erase the shadow of his presence from her flat.

'Isabella…'

The low growl was a warning not to try his patience further.

'It is late and I have no wish to make a public spectacle of myself by discussing what should be a very private matter between a husband and wife in the street like this. You will get into my car and I will drive you to your house—'

'I will...you will,' Isabelle tossed in, imitating the autocratic tone of his command with bitter satire. 'Whatever happened to please and thank you, Luis? Or does your lordship not use such courtesies with the peasants?'

His breath hissed in between his teeth, warning her that he was very close to losing his grip on his barely reined-in temper.

'*Please,*' he said with a sarcasm that matched her own. 'Isabelle, I just want to talk.'

'But it's what you want to talk about that worries me. You'll have to tell me more than that, Luis, or I'm not going anywhere with you.'

'*Muy bien!*'

His hands flew up in a gesture that was a perfect blend of exasperation and resignation.

'All right! We will do it your way if that's what you prefer! The reason I am here, Isabella, is because...'

'Because you want to end our marriage,' Isabelle supplied unhappily when he paused, seeming uncharacteristically at a loss for words. 'You don't have to spell it out, Luis. I sent you that letter, after all. I guessed from the start that you were here to arrange for our divorce.'

'Then you guessed wrong, *querida*. Totally wrong. I have not come here looking for a divorce. On the contrary, I am here because I want you to come back to me.'

CHAPTER TWO

'I WANT you to come back to me.'

When she had been expecting something so totally different, the words made no sense at all to her.

'Come—back?' she managed through shock-stiffened lips. 'I don't…'

'Come back, as in return to me.'

Luis sighed his exasperation.

'You are, after all, my wife.'

But when she still stared at him, blank-faced, her eyes looking bruised, he elaborated further.

'I want you to come to Spain with me as my wife. *Madre de Dios*, I did not think that my English was so—'

'It's not that!' Isabelle protested sharply, still unable to believe what she had heard. 'Your English is perfect and you know it. It's just that I can't see what you want with me.'

'I need you.'

And he hated himself for saying it. That much was there in the tight clench of his jaw, the way the words had to be forced out past lips that would clearly rather be saying anything else.

'Why?'

'Do I have to explain here?'

He was every inch the arrogant aristocrat once again, proud head flung back, eyes flashing. She would have sworn that even his nostrils flared in an expression of disapproval.

'You certainly have to explain. Where you do it is immaterial to me.'

'Then we will go to your house.'

'Oh, no…' That was not what she had meant.

'Isabella, what I would like right now is to get inside and out of this wind. This damn northern climate is so very different from what I am used to and I need a cup of coffee.'

His shiver was exaggerated for effect, deliberately so, she knew, a reluctant smile pulling at the corners of her mouth.

If he had wanted to appeal straight to her heart, using the tug of shared memory, then he couldn't have chosen a more effective way of doing so. Luis had always hated the colder climate of Yorkshire as opposed to the warmth of his native Andalucia and had complained bitterly about it. So now his gesture, his expression, his tone of voice, all revived images of him doing just the same in far happier times.

And he knew it, damn him! She was sure he had planned it this way.

'Oh, all right.'

What was she hesitating for anyway? she asked herself. If there really was a chance of the two of them getting back together, then she wanted to know about it. She wanted to hear what he was going to say and find out just why he had changed his mind. So why did it matter *where* they talked?

'We'll go to my place. You said you have a car?'

Of course he had a car. A sleek, powerful, softly growling monster of a vehicle that she couldn't even name. But she knew that she was sitting in the financial equivalent of the mortgage on her flat—and then some. Luis de Silva loved speed, he loved luxury, and as a result he only ever had the very best of everything.

Which begged the question why was he here, like this, with her? A man like Luis, with the title he possessed, the fortune that was his to command, could have had anyone. All he had to do was to click his fingers and women fell into line, just waiting for him to pick them. There must have been dozens in the years since she had last seen him. Rich, sophisticated, beautiful women, like Catalina, the only one of his former lovers she had ever met. Women who would have been only too happy to grace his life, be photographed on his arm, warm his bed...

The sudden shiver that ran down her spine at the thought made her twist nervously in her seat.

'Turn left here.'

Her voice was strained and tight with the emotions she was

struggling to hold back, and she made herself stare straight ahead, forcing away the hot, bitter tears that threatened. She would *not* let them fall!

'Go right to the end of the street. It's the last house.'

'I know.'

The quiet comment stunned her, making her heart stop dead in astonishment. But then she remembered.

'You said I didn't answer my door… You've been here before?'

His dark head moved in a curt nod.

'You've been watching me!'

'You said you'd been away,' he explained with overly patient reasonableness. 'I could hardly watch you if you weren't there. Where did you go?'

'To Lynette's. If you remember, she…'

No, reminding him of her friend was a bad mistake. Talking about Lynette meant turning his thoughts towards Rob, Lynn's brother-in-law, and the man Luis thought she'd betrayed him with. The reason why he'd walked out on their brief marriage years before.

'You can park here,' she muttered hastily.

Luis swung the car to the side of the road with a suddenness that had her glancing at him in surprise. This husband of hers usually prided himself on his driving, handling his expensive vehicles with practised skill. The mention of Lynn had changed the atmosphere in the car. The tension between them had thickened suddenly until it was almost impossible for her to breathe.

'I'll go and open the door,' she said, scrambling inelegantly in her haste to be out of the car. 'That way you won't have to stand out in the cold too long.'

Luis watched her walk up the short path to the lighted porch, willing himself to calm down, to get a grip on himself. Strong fingers drummed a restless tattoo on the rim of the steering wheel in an outward expression of the inner turmoil of his thoughts.

The drive from the city centre had been a particularly sophisticated sort of torment, with every cell in his body reacting urgently and painfully to the presence of Isabelle's slim form so close to his after all this time.

She was so familiar and yet so unknown. *Dios!* She still wore the same perfume as she had done then, the mixture of rose and sandalwood tantalising his nostrils and making him harden instantly. And then, while he'd still been struggling to control the hungry need that simply being with her had sparked off, she had had to mention Lynette Michaels.

'*No!*'

He muttered the word aloud as he pulled his key from the ignition and pushed the door open. He would not think about it. Wouldn't even let the memory of Rob Michaels into his thoughts. If that happened then he would turn and leave, heading away from here like a bat out of hell.

So he made himself walk down the road towards her, follow her into the small, narrow hallway. He watched in astonishment as she took out another key and pushed it into the first door on the right.

'What? You have a *flat* here?'

Her face was turned to him sharply, confusion stamped clearly on it.

'Of course—what did you think? You didn't think I owned the whole house, did you?'

'I thought…I sent you money.'

'I didn't want your money.'

'Evidently.'

The door was open now and those golden tiger's eyes were scanning the small, slightly shabby room, taking in the deep brown, well-worn settee and chairs, the equally elderly table and dresser. The only saving graces in what was a rather ugly place were the clean, freshly painted cream walls, and the pretty floral-patterned curtains and cushion covers. Isabelle had made those herself in an attempt to brighten the place up.

'I would have kept you better than this.'

'You wouldn't have *kept* me at all, Luis! I can look after myself. And you made it only too plain that you never wanted to see me again, that you wanted me out of your life for good.'

'And does that surprise you? You slept with another man while you were married to me.'

'I did no such thing. I *didn't*!' she emphasised as he eyed her sceptically, obvious disbelief darkening his eyes. 'It never happened, Luis.'

Was he listening to her? He *had* to listen to her!

Two years before, he had refused even to hear a word she'd tried to say. He'd simply turned and walked out of her life without a backward glance. He had cut himself off from her so completely that it had been as if he had vanished off the face of the earth. Her phone calls had gone unanswered, her letters had been returned unopened.

That was why, in the end, she had resorted to sending him a solicitor's letter telling him that she wanted to legalise their separation. It had been the most painful decision she had ever had to make.

'I didn't do it. I was innocent of everything you accused me of. I don't know what happened. I don't know how Rob got there.'

He almost believed her. When she turned that pleading face on him, green eyes wide, the disturbing thing was that the sudden kick of his heart told him that he was still weak enough for it to matter. That, blind stupid fool that he was, he *wanted* to believe her.

But that was forgetting that she was an actress. That she had spent years training to do just this. To deceive an audience into believing that what she did, what she said, was the truth. He had seen her act, knew how good she was at it. But he had never expected to see that skill of hers turned against him.

'Luis, you have to understand…'

He had hesitated just long enough to light a tiny flame of hope inside her. A hope that flickered, steadied, grew for a moment…then died painfully abruptly as he shook his dark head, scowling savagely.

'I *have* to do nothing!' he snarled.

But then, another second later, a disturbing change came over his face. The burn of anger disappeared from his eyes, leaving them cold and opaque, and his shrug was cool, totally indifferent. And Isabelle found that even more frightening than his icy rage.

'It doesn't matter. It's in the past. It doesn't affect the present.'

'But it has to.'

'I told you, there is no "has to" about this.'

Another pause, even more deliberate this time. The bronze eyes watched her coldly, assessing her like some specimen on a laboratory table, one he was just about to dissect.

'You have to understand about that night—'

'What *you* have to understand,' Luis inserted in a savage undertone, 'is that you are wearing my patience very thin. I do not want to talk about that night—and if you are wise, then neither will you! Why do you persist in this?'

'In—in what?'

'In reminding me of that night—of all nights? Do you want to make me think of it—remember every disgusting detail? Do you want to etch it even more clearly in my mind so that I cannot forget it? Believe me, *mi belleza*, if you do that then you are risking my turning round and walking out of here and never coming back.'

'No—please...' Not a second time.

'If you want me to stay,' he swept on furiously, overriding her whispered protest, 'then you would do better to help me forget. Never to mention it again and let the memory fade. Otherwise I can never take you back—my pride would not allow it.'

'And can you do that? Can you really put it to the back of your mind?'

She didn't believe he could. How could he push away all memory of that appalling night when the anger, the betrayal he must have felt then had kept him apart from her ever since? And as for his stubborn pride, she really couldn't imagine that he could swallow it hard enough to start over again.

'Can you pretend it never happened and let us have a new beginning?'

He had to struggle with himself to answer her. The fight he

was having was there in the taut, drawn lines of his face, the tension in his jaw, the darkness of his eyes.

'I have to,' he said flatly, all emotion drained from his voice.

'What?' She couldn't believe she'd heard him right. 'Luis—what did you say?'

But his mood had changed again.

'I believe you offered me coffee.'

And that was clearly as much as she was going to get from him, for now at least.

'Of course. But first let me try and make things more comfortable in here.'

He watched silently as she lit the small, spluttering gas fire.

'Do you want to take off your coat? It will get warmer—eventually.'

And she might feel a little easier, more able to talk, if he didn't look as if staying was the last thing on his mind. As if he was about to get up and walk out at the soonest possible opportunity.

'Do you promise me that?'

She remembered that dry tone of old, her heart jerking in her breast at the memory. And the bitter-sweet sensations were intensified sharply as he shrugged himself out of his coat and handed it to her. The jacket was of the finest, softest wool, still warm from the heat of his body, and the scent of the subtle cologne he wore rose from the expensive fabric, tormenting her with the memories it evoked.

'W-well, I wouldn't move too far away from it.'

It was the first time she had really seen him in the light and, having looked once, she found it impossible to drag her eyes away from him again. He had always had this effect on her. Had always possessed a hard-core sexuality that produced a kick like a mule in the pit of her stomach.

The worst thing was that he was completely unaware of it. He never even considered the effect that sleek black hair, gleaming bronze eyes and smooth olive skin might have on the opposite sex. And when his naturally dramatic colouring was combined with a fiercely carved bone structure, all angles and planes, hard chin and a devastatingly sensual mouth, then the whole effect was as potent as a crate of explosives.

There were new lines on his stunning face, etched there more by experience than the passage of time. She knew of the death of his brother a year before, and her heart ached for the loss he must have felt. He and Diego had always been so close, almost like twins rather than siblings separated by four and a half years in age. Luis would have missed his older brother terribly.

'I—I'll make the coffee!' she said, as much to persuade herself to move as to inform him of anything.

Unnervingly, he prowled after her, coming to lounge in the narrow doorway, one broad shoulder propped against the frame. Just knowing he was there made Isabelle's hands shake as she filled the kettle, splashing water everywhere. He was too big, too strong, too dark—too *much*, especially when in the confines of her tiny kitchen. Prickling awareness fizzed over her skin, making her heart lurch into a rapid staccato beat.

'So what brought about this change of—of attitude?'

'Change of heart' didn't describe it properly. There seemed to be no bit of his *heart* involved in the decision to take her back, if the bald, blunt declaration he had made was anything to go by.

'It's not so much—Isabella—*atención*!'

It was hard and sharp, sounding a note of warning, and it froze her to the spot.

'What?'

The word was still on her tongue when Luis grabbed her, powerful hands clamping tight over her arms, and twisted her around and away from the stove. The movement took her into his arms, close up against the hard wall of his chest so that she gasped in sudden shock, not sure whether it was the unexpectedness of his reaction or the pounding of her heart as a result of being so close to him that was making her feel this way.

'L-Luis… What are you doing?'

Her voice sharpened as she felt his hands at her throat, fumbling for and finding the clasp that held the long, swirling cloak fastened.

'No, Isabella.'

Roughly he pushed her restraining fingers aside, his dark head bent, attention totally on what he was doing. With an impatient movement he snapped it open, tossing the garment aside with an impatient exclamation.

'Hey, that…'

Her protest died as she suddenly saw why he had reacted as he had. On one side of the cloak, just at the edge, a long, brown mark showed where the flames from the gas ring had caught it, scorching it to the point where a ragged hole had appeared in the fabric. Another couple of seconds and it would have been alight.

'Oh—no…'

All the strength seemed to leave her legs at the thought of what might have happened. Visions of the cloak catching fire, the flames taking hold, engulfed her thoughts. She could have been so badly burned.

'Luis, thank you…'

Or perhaps the way she was feeling had nothing to do with what might have happened, but rather just what *was* happening now.

His arm was tight around her waist, supporting her with easy strength. She was so close that she could hear the thud of his heart beneath the soft material of his shirt, feel the way his chest rose and fell with every breath, inhale the intensely personal scent of his skin.

And everything stilled, held immobile.

'Luis…'

She was back where she had been in the past. Back where she belonged. In his arms, held close. And it felt so right. So very, very right.

A tiny adjustment of her position, a small twist of her body, brought them to face each other. Breast to chest, pelvis to pelvis, legs tight against the muscular length of his.

'Luis…'

He should never have taken off that damn cloak, Luis told

himself furiously. Should never have exposed himself to temptation like this!

Oh, it had been bad enough before. Simply seeing her face, the blonde sheen of her hair, the emerald brilliance of her eyes had been hard enough. The sound of her voice, soft and slightly husky in his ears, had awoken memories best left buried. It had set his pulses thudding, reminded him of hunger he preferred not to recall.

But now...

'What happened to us?'

It was just the faintest thread of sound, so thin that without thinking he dropped his head instinctively to catch her hesitant words.

And immediately regretted it.

His cheek was now lying against the softness of her hair and the temptation to turn, just so, and press his lips to the silky strands was almost more than he could resist. The scent of her body rose towards his nostrils, flowers and rain; the sweet, subtle aroma of her skin, tormented him with the recollection of how it had once been so that his body stirred, hardened, demanded. His senses were swimming, swirling on a warm sea of desire, and deep inside the hunger of physical need clawed at him remorselessly.

He couldn't fight it any longer. Couldn't hold back, couldn't hide the way she affected him.

Slowly his proud head lowered, and, sensing his intention, Isabelle lifted her own face to his, her mouth softening, lips parting instinctively in anticipation of his kiss.

Behind them the kettle, knocked off the flames by being moved slightly to one side, came to the boil again with a wild shriek. Startled and confused, Isabelle took a step backwards, blinking in shock.

'*Por Dios!*' Luis muttered, darkly savage, though whether he was swearing at her, the kettle, or himself, Isabelle had no way of knowing.

She didn't have time to decide before he had wrenched himself away from her, releasing her arms with a speed that made it look as if he feared it might actually contaminate him to keep hold of her.

'Luis...' she tried, but the moment was gone, destroyed in a second, and there was no way she could get it back.

But it had happened. And the fact that it had told her something very deep and very important about this husband of hers. Something she was sure that he would have preferred to keep totally secret. That he would have died rather than have her find out.

'Where's the coffee?' Luis snapped, snatching the kettle up off the stove. 'Mugs?'

'Here...'

Isabelle obeyed the note of command in his tone automatically, but her thoughts weren't on the simple task at hand. Instead they were centred on those few moments in Luis's arms and the seconds when she had *known*, when on the deepest, most intuitive level of understanding, she had sensed just what had been happening to him.

He still wanted her.

He might try to deny it to her face. Might act as if he were totally indifferent to her, but the truth was something else.

He couldn't hide the reaction of his body. And she had felt the hard, hot response that had revealed the desire he couldn't control. But it was more than that. In the moment she had looked into his eyes, she had seen the dark, fierce blaze of something very strong and very primitive. Something more potent than thought and more forceful than any attempt at restraint.

And she knew she could use that against him to try and discover the truth about how he really felt.

CHAPTER THREE

'SHALL we take our coffee into the other room?'

Luis didn't look at Isabelle as he spoke, already heading into the small sitting room. He needed to put some space between them. He had to regain control of his senses, force his clamouring body under control before he could take things any further.

'The fire must have warmed the place up by now.'

He had known he was lost in the seconds that he had tossed aside the enveloping cloak, and seen her standing before him, tall and slender in the clinging green velvet dress. Long and flowing, it shaped her delicate ribcage, the narrowness of her waist, with sensual intimacy, hugged tight by the elaborately embroidered belt.

The colour did amazing things to her skin and hair, making her eyes gleam like polished emeralds, the soft flush of her cheeks matched by the lush curve of her mouth. And standing so close, inches taller than she was, he had had the best view possible of the warm curves of her breasts, the opulent cleavage created by the corsetry of the boned bodice.

She'd filled out in the years since he'd last seen her. She was no longer just a girl burgeoning into maturity, but a woman in her prime. Stunning, sexy and enticing.

And he wanted her.

Dios, he wanted her more than he had ever wanted any woman in his life. More than the sensual madness that had pushed him towards her in the first moments that they had met. More than the aching hunger that had made him propose marriage far too soon, and well before either of them had actually been ready.

'It still isn't all that warm in here.'

Deliberately, Isabelle came to sit beside him on the small

119

settee, curling her legs up underneath her in a way that brought her even closer to him.

'We need to sit right in front of the fire,' she added by way of a belated excuse for her action. 'So—now I think you owe me an explanation of why you're here.'

'I've explained.'

He was definitely on the run, mentally at least. Those copper-coloured eyes wouldn't look directly at her, but stared straight into the small gas fire. And the long, lean body was held unnaturally taut, as far away from her as was possible on the two-seater settee, making her determined to press home the advantage he had unexpectedly given her.

'I told you, I want you to be my wife again. If you do, then you'll want for nothing. You'll live in luxury; you'll only have to think of something you'd like and it will be yours.'

'And you think that will be enough?'

Heavy lids dropped down hastily over gleaming bronze eyes, hiding their expression from her.

'What else could you want?'

Deliberately Isabelle leaned nearer, almost but not quite touching him.

'Is this to be a proper marriage, Luis? A *real* marriage?'

'Of course.'

She ran her tongue over her lips with slow provocation and watched as his gaze darkened, his pupils widening in response.

'But—we might not be—compatible.'

Luis's response was a short, hard bark of laughter.

'Not compatible! Oh, Isabella, *mi esposa*, you cannot think that. That *compatibility* was the one thing that brought us together. The thing that never died between us. It will still be there. You need have no fear of that.'

'Would you like to prove that?'

There it was again. That sudden stiffening of the muscular frame, the wariness in his eyes. He might act the hard, invulnerable, untouchable male, but every once in a while something flickered in that polished amber gaze, revealing a hidden emotion he couldn't quite conceal.

But what was that emotion?

Isabelle leaned even closer, looked deep into those dark, watchful eyes.

'Why don't you kiss me, Luis?'

Luis stilled suddenly and the narrow-eyed glance he shot her was sharp, assessing, full of suspicion.

'What is this, *belleza*?' he demanded harshly. 'Are you planning on seduction?'

She tried a smile to disarm him but even she could feel it wavering at the corners.

'You're going to have to do it some time. That is, if we're to have this proper marriage.'

'Oh, I see. This is a way of saying yes without actually admitting that you're giving in?'

'It might be.'

'Isabella…'

It was a growl of warning, impatient and rough, making her stomach clench in sudden apprehension. But she'd started this. She had to go on—right to the finish.

'I'll tell you what…'

She tried to pitch her voice at a huskily seductive level and knew that she had succeeded as she saw the flare of response deep in his eyes.

'Why don't you kiss me and we'll see? If what you say is true—if that *compatibility* is still there, then maybe I will agree to your terms.'

And she would know from the way he kissed her whether she was deceiving herself totally or not.

Her mouth was almost touching his now, and the sweet scent of her skin surrounded him, awakening every cell in his body, sending the hot, honeyed pulse of desire raging along his veins. He couldn't have resisted her if he'd tried.

And he didn't want to try.

One kiss, he told himself fiercely. One kiss and one kiss only. Just enough to prove to himself that he wasn't the fool he feared he was where this woman was concerned.

'*Está bien!*' he muttered roughly, reaching out and closing his hands hard over the fine bones of her shoulders.

With a rough, jerking movement he pulled her towards him

in the same moment that his head came down and his mouth fastened over hers. He took her lips with such force that they opened involuntarily under his, giving him access to a more intimate invasion.

She gave a small, gasping sigh into his mouth as her tongue met his and her hands slid up to tangle in the raven silk of his hair, pulling his head down even further, to deepen and prolong the kiss.

And in that second he knew he was helpless. Knew that he could no more deny his feelings than he could tear himself away from her. His heart was racing, his breath coming in raw, uneven snatches, his head swimming under the sensual onslaught of the passion that blazed deep inside.

His body was hard and tight, his need so intense it was a burning pain. He couldn't get her close enough, couldn't touch her enough, his hands moving restlessly over her slender frame, stroking, caressing, feeling. Yearning fingers closed over the thrusting curves of her breasts and his breath caught roughly in his throat.

'Luis…'

It was a moan of response against her lips and she crushed herself even closer, pushing the warm weight of her flesh into his cupped palms.

'*Dios*, Isabella, *mi belleza*…'

All his English had deserted him. He couldn't have formed a single word in any language but his own to save his life. He couldn't think, could only feel, only knew that if he didn't possess her here, now, this very second, he would die from wanting…

Isabelle felt as if her bones were melting in the heat of her desire. She had lost track of just why she had started this in the first place, only knew that it felt right, perfect, the most natural thing in the world. The *only* thing in the world she wanted.

She shifted slightly on the settee as Luis pulled at the enfolding weight of the velvet skirt, tugging it upwards. Her heart seemed to beat high up in her throat as he slid hot fingers up the length of her legs and along the soft whiteness of her thighs to the spot where the sharpest pulse of hunger throbbed in aching need, then slowly, agonisingly, away again.

'You want to know why I'm here,' he muttered against her mouth. 'Well, I'll tell you. I'm here because when I got that letter I realised there was no way I could let you go. In all the time we've been apart, no woman has ever had the effect on me that you had. I can't eat—I can't sleep for wanting you. I haven't lived these past years, couldn't rest until I had you back in my arms, in my bed. And then when I saw you again—just one look was all it took to revive the old feelings—the hunger, the desire...'

He paused, looked deep into her eyes, then lifted one hand to trail the backs of his fingers slowly down the side of her face, his darkened gaze holding her mesmerised as he did so.

'And I know you're feeling the same.'

'Yes...'

She didn't even think of trying to deny it. Each tiny touch had triggered off explosions of desire along every nerve in her body. It was as if she were a ready-laid fire, primed with finest kindling, dust-dry logs. All it needed was the spark of a single match to set light to everything, send the flames of passion roaring through her, drying her mouth so that she licked nervously at painfully parched lips.

'Yes,' she croaked again. 'That's exactly the way I've been feeling.'

The way she was leaning towards him was inviting him to do exactly the same. The way she was looking at him was like a magnet, drawing him closer and closer. The way her mouth had softened, her lips parting, was an open invitation for his kiss again.

And Luis took it without hesitation.

His hands came out, slid round the back of her neck, up into the golden fall of her hair. The pressure of their hold brought her face to his, angling her head so that their mouths fitted perfectly together.

This time, the first touch of his lips was gentle, almost tentative, searching, questioning. But when her response gave him the answer he sought without restraint, then the kiss soon turned into a powerful, crushing demand.

And she met that too. Met it and matched it, moving from following to leading in the space of an urgent, pounding heartbeat. Her kiss told its own story of longing and hunger, of giving him of herself and taking everything he offered.

And when, with their mouths still locked together, he stood up, strong arms taking her upright with him, she knew exactly what he had in mind because it was what was in her thoughts too. She went with him, willingly and gladly, her heart recognising that this was what she wanted most in all the world.

He half walked, half carried her towards the bedroom, finding it by instinct, his lips still taking hers, tasting, giving, promising all kinds of delights ahead of them. The silence in the room was total, the only sound the pounding of their two hearts in total unison, in complete accord with each other.

There was no need for speech; no need for words. His hands told her she was beautiful as they touched and tantalised, smoothing, caressing, arousing, communicating perfectly the way he saw her. And his body proclaimed his need for her as it strained against hers, hard and demanding, fiercely aroused. He was awe-inspiring in his strength and the power of his passion, and yet she felt totally safe, completely at one with him.

Because the same hunger was burning its way through her. It made her body tremble with need as Luis's strong hands found the zip fastening of her dress, slid it right down to the base of her spine so that all she had to do was to let her hands drop and the green velvet slithered to the floor, pooling at her feet. The fine lace of her slip, the sliver of satin that was her bra followed, removed and tossed to the floor in a series of intent, unhurried movements that spoke eloquently of his powerful restraint.

Isabelle could feel no such thing. With his mouth still working its sensual magic on her, her whole body clenched in a paroxysm of anticipation, a trembling longing for more. She was clinging to him now, her legs no longer capable of supporting her as he swung her up into his arms and slowly lowered her onto the downy quilt on the bed.

'Isabella, *amada...belleza...*'

It was an incantation of longing against her skin, his mouth kissing its way from her lips, over her throat, her shoulder, and down the length of her body. Isabelle caught her breath in sharply as his lips touched the slope of her breast, brushed the pink swollen nipple, but didn't linger. Instead they slid lower, over the tautened muscles of her stomach, his tongue briefly circling the shallow indentation of her navel.

'Luis...' she breathed, needing to say his name, then choked into silence again as knowing hands eased the sliver of satin that was her only covering down the length of her legs, his tormenting mouth following it all the way.

Only then did he pause to throw off his own clothes, dropping them carelessly wherever they fell, and sliding down onto the bed beside her, gathering her into the heat of his body.

And now his kisses were fiercer, thrilling in their demand. His touch had lost that careful restraint, becoming instead the urgent, hungry caress of a man close to the edge of his control. Long, tanned fingers closed over the thrust of her breasts, taking their weight into the warmth of his palms. His thumbs stroked over the creamy curves, encircling the swollen peaks until she moaned aloud in agonised delight and arched her back against the support of the pillows behind her.

'I've waited so long for this,' Luis muttered against her heated skin. 'So long—too long. A lifetime, it seems.'

'Too long,' Isabelle echoed on a sigh that broke into a high-pitched cry of delight as his mouth took the place of his hands, his tongue tracing the same tormenting path as his thumb had followed just seconds before. 'Too long...'

'But now there will be no more waiting...no more time. Now you are back where you belong...in my bed...'

'Yes...'

It was a cry of affirmation, a sob of ecstasy as his lips closed over her nipple, drawing it into the heat of this mouth and suckling hard. The stinging sensation of delight made her writhe frantically beneath the imprisoning weight of his body, her head twisting from side to side on the pillows. She closed her eyes tight, the better to concentrate on the sensation that spread throughout her body. Every pleasure spot she possessed seemed to be linked in a burning golden chain of arousal, all of it centred on and radiating out from that one core point of her being.

And the hunger between her legs was a throbbing need that had her shifting restlessly, moaning her need, incapable of putting what she wanted into speech.

But Luis had no need of words, no need for instruction. He interpreted her needs, anticipated them with the intuitive instinct of a lover. His fingers slid through the moist curls at the most feminine core of her body, stroking her intimately, a rough growl of satisfaction sounding in his throat as he discovered just how hungry for him she was.

'*Querida... Mi mujer...*'

All his English deserted him. He could manage only his native Spanish, the words rough and incoherent, muttered in a voice that was thick and raw with need.

'*Amada...amada...*'

His voice thick with passion, his eyes blazing, a wash of dark colour marking the sculpted lines of his cheekbones, he pushed her legs apart and inserted his long body between them.

Isabelle lifted her hips to meet the force of his invasion, opening to him, welcoming him, drawing him as deeply into her as she could manage, and she heard his wild cry of satisfaction as the hot silk of her closed about him.

For a second, simply lying there was enough. Simply knowing he was with her, inside her, filling her, was satisfaction after all the long, lonely days, months, years, of being without him. But in the space of a heavy, thudding heartbeat that satisfaction changed into a new desire, desire into demand, and she began to move underneath him.

'Isabella,' he choked. '*Mi mujer...*'

Hard hands clamped down on her shoulders, holding her still, as he took charge of their lovemaking, slowly at first, then faster, harder, stronger. His passion-lit gaze burned down into hers, his head thrown back, his jaw tight, as he lost control. The hot, fierce thrusts grew wilder, more forceful, taking both of them higher and higher until at last, with a harsh cry, he put his arms around her, gathering her up to him, and his lips crushed hers as they lost all connection with reality and the world splintered around them.

It was the start of a long, hot night. When eventually Isabelle focused again, she just lay, letting her breathing slow, her heart stop racing to the point of bursting. Beside her, she heard Luis stir, sigh with weary satisfaction and stretch lazily.

'You okay?' he questioned softly, his accent very pronounced, his voice husky.

'More than okay,' Isabelle answered dreamily. 'Much more than okay.'

At that point she must have drifted into sleep because the next time she opened her eyes it was as Luis slid from the bed and padded silently across the thick carpet heading for the bathroom.

As Isabelle lay in drowsy contentment, she heard the sound of the shower being turned on, water splashing onto the tiles. The next moment Luis was back, easing the quilt from her lazy body, lifting her in his arms.

'Hey…what are you doing?'

It was a feeble attempt at a protest because the truth was she didn't care. As long as he was there, with her, with the warm satin of his body against hers, the strength of his arms enclosing her, the scent of his skin in her nostrils, he could do anything he liked and she wouldn't complain.

'Don't panic,' he murmured, shouldering open the glass door and carrying her inside the cubicle. 'I just thought you'd like a shower.'

Hiding a smile against the strength of his shoulder, Isabelle injected a mock protest into her voice.

'Do I have to? It sounds rather over-energetic to me.'

His laughter was low, full of genuine amusement, sounding deep inside the powerful chest against which her cheek rested.

'Trust me, *mi angel*, you won't have to do a thing. Just leave everything up to me.'

He was as good as his word. From the moment that he lowered her feet to the floor so that she was under the flow of the heated water, he took charge of everything. Isabelle didn't even have to find the strength to stand upright as he supported her on one muscular arm, lathering scented shower gel all over her acquiescent body with his free hand.

'Mmm, that feels good.'

Eyes closed, she edged round until she was leaning back against him, the soft hairs on his chest brushing the sensitive skin between her shoulder blades, her buttocks fitting snugly against his pelvis. With two hands available now, the pleasure of his massage more than doubled, long, caressing sweeps of his firm fingers alternating with gentler, deliberately lingering strokes over her breasts and dipping down between her legs.

'Don't stop,' she begged. 'Please don't stop.'

She didn't know at what stage simple pleasure turned to hunger, at what point hunger became desire. She only knew that the firm pressure of Luis's fingers sliding all over her skin was a delicious torment that woke every one of her senses and set them clamouring all over again.

And it was only too obvious that Luis felt the same. The heated pressure of his aroused body against hers was the last straw, driving all thought of restraint from her mind. Twisting round again, she pressed herself close to him, lacing her arms around his neck.

'I want you now,' she whispered in his ear, her words half drowned by the rushing water. 'Right here. Right now.'

His sigh was both a sound of delight and surrender to a force that was stronger than either of them.

'Your wish is my command, *querida...*'

The next moment she was lifted off her feet, her legs encircling his narrow waist, her back against the steam-damp tiled wall. He thrust into her with a guttural sound deep in his throat, his mouth closing over hers, his tongue echoing the more intimate invasion of her body.

It was hard and hot and fast and gloriously fulfilling. The water pounded down on their heads, its heat and pressure adding to the tumult of sensations ricocheting through Isabelle's wildly excited body. She had never climaxed so fast, so fiercely, never been so totally out of control. And when it was over both of them sagged against the walls of the cubicle, struggling for the return of some sort of reality.

She was only vaguely aware of the moment Luis finally reached up a hand and switched off the shower. Of him wrapping her in a thick, soft towel and taking her with him back into the bedroom. Drying her tenderly as a mother, he carried her to the bed, laid her down and pulled the downy quilt up over her exhausted form.

The faintly cool touch of the covers roused her slightly and she caught at his hand when he would have eased away.

'Don't go! Don't leave me.'

'Leave, *amada*? Never. This is just the start of things. We've only just begun.'

Already sleep was claiming her, rolling through her mind like mist coming in from the sea, but she knew the moment he joined her in the bed, felt the heat of his long, powerful body, the strength of the arm that came round her waist, pulling her close up against him.

'Sleep for now, *querida*,' he murmured, pressing a swift, soft kiss on her cheek. 'And when you wake I'll still be here. I'll always be here. I'm never going to let you go again.'

Another kiss, more lingering this time, landed on her hair, and the arm that held her tightened.

'Now you know *exactly* why I want you back. You're mine. We belong together. Tonight has proved that.'

'We belong together.' The words gave her hope. Hope that if she spent more time with Luis, if she went back to living as his wife, they might just have a future together. 'There was no way I could let you go,' he had said.

It was enough. When she had believed that he would never want her anywhere near him again, it was more than enough. It was a beginning. Something to build the possibility of a future on. They had a long way to go, but they had taken the first steps.

In the darkness Luis stretched lazily, lying on his back, with one hand behind his head, staring up at the ceiling as he let the tides of sleep wash over him.

His body ached with a bone-deep satisfaction, his clamouring senses stilled for a while at least. At his side Isabelle lay, deeply asleep, her slim body softly curved towards his. He would let her sleep for now. There would be plenty of time to talk—and more—in the morning.

A wide grin spread across his expressive mouth and he stretched again, sighing in deep, luxurious contentment. Things might work out after all. Whatever had happened in the past was the past. Isabelle was here, with him now—and surely she couldn't have responded to him as she had tonight if there was anyone else in her life?

But one way or another, he was determined there was no going back. Isabelle was his wife, and she was here to stay.

Turning over on his side, he draped a possessive arm around his wife's still form, closed his eyes, and fell deeply asleep.

CHAPTER FOUR

THE weather in Andalucia was totally different from the cool winds and miserable, drizzling rain they had left behind in Yorkshire. As Isabelle alighted from the powerful car that had taken them on the last stage of their journey she stepped out into warm, bright sunshine and only the gentlest of delicate breezes.

But somehow the warmth didn't seem to reach inside her. It brushed over her skin, the breeze tangled in her hair, but it didn't touch her heart, which remained as fearful and uncertain as ever.

Should she really be here? Was she doing the right thing?

Last night she had been so sure. She had been so confident that a new beginning was possible. But were the feelings that she had experienced in the heat of their lovemaking and its aftermath enough to carry them through into that new beginning?

What was it that people said about the cold light of dawn?

She had woken that morning to find that Luis was already up and dressed, bending over her to place a brief kiss on her sleepy face.

'What? Where are you going?'

'To get my things; check out of the hotel. Then I'll be back.'

'So you are coming back?' Her heart jolted in a mixture of uncertainty and delight.

'Do you doubt it? Oh, yes, *querida*. I'm coming back. I think last night rather proved a point.'

'What point?' She couldn't get her sleep-clouded mind to focus and frowned in confusion.

'"Why don't you kiss me and we'll see?"' he quoted, his tone laced with a dark humour. '"If that compatibility is still there, then maybe I will agree to your terms."'

Eyes gleaming with appreciation raked the length of her slim body from the tousled golden hair, down over the pale skin of her face and neck, still marked red in places by the demanding force of his kisses.

'Made up your mind, then, have you, sweetheart? Because if you haven't, then I certainly have.'

Bending suddenly, taking her totally by surprise, he pressed his lips to hers once more, and she could feel his smile against her mouth as she was unable to control her instant, passionate response.

'I think we'd both agree that that *compatibility* is still there, *querida*. So you don't have to say another word. I'll take that as a yes.'

Her tongue seemed too swollen, too clumsy to answer him, but he clearly didn't need her to say a single thing. Snatching up his jacket, he slung it over his shoulder and headed for the door.

'I'll give you an hour or so to pack,' he tossed at her, not even sparing a backward glance. 'I'll be here to pick you up on my way to the airport.'

She had packed as she'd been commanded to do, but all the time her body had been tight with tension, never knowing quite whether to believe that Luis would come back or not. And so she had jumped like a startled cat when the sound of his hard fist hitting the scuffed and faded wood of the front door had had her hurrying to let him in before he splintered the lock.

'Do you think you could make a little more noise?' she'd demanded, hiding her private feelings behind a mask of annoyance. 'There are people still asleep in the house, you know.'

'At this time?'

His brief, impatient glance at his watch expressed irritated disapproval without a word having to be spoken.

'Some of the guys who live here work shifts. We don't all have the luxury of being able to come and go as we please. Some of us have to earn our livings.'

'In Spain I would have put in a couple of hours' work at the vineyard already.'

Luis dismissed her protest with an arrogant flick of his hand. 'I prefer to be out and busy before the heat of the day sets in.'

'Which is fine in Spain, but not exactly appropriate here,' Isabelle retorted with a reluctant glance out at the rain-soaked street. 'We don't get a chance to take a siesta and rest for half the afternoon.'

She realised her mistake as soon as the words had left her mouth, anything else she might have been about to say disappearing in a tangle of confusion as she saw the wicked, glinting glance he shot her from behind dark lashes.

'As I recall, we didn't exactly use the time for *resting*,' he drawled sardonically, the gleam in his eyes growing as he watched the hot colour race up her neck and into her face, until she was almost exactly the same bright pink as the cotton jumper and cardigan she wore with loose oatmeal trousers for comfort in travelling.

'No—like every man, you only had one thing on your mind,' she retorted tartly, too knocked off balance mentally to care that that was exactly the wrong thing to say, giving Luis an opening that he would be unable to resist.

He didn't disappoint her.

'Every man?' His tone had sharpened perceptibly. 'Am I to take it you're talking about Rob Michaels here?'

There, his name was out in the open. The thing that had come between them, broken them apart, had been acknowledged at last.

'You can take it that I'm talking about whoever you want, whatever you want! But seeing as last night you were the one who was so insistent that I never mention that man's name again so that we could let the memory fade, don't you think it's rather hypocritical of you to bring him into the conversation again at the first opportunity?'

His answer was a fierce, savage glare, one that turned his eyes molten gold with fury, but she told herself to ignore it.

'After all, you were the one who invited your ex-mistress along on what was supposed to be a private party in that hotel.'

'Catalina invited herself along,' Luis snapped. 'What did you expect me to do? Tell the hotel she wasn't allowed to book in? I thought she'd be company for you.'

'And I wouldn't have needed company if you'd not taken yourself off to London. I was miserable. I had a cold and it was my birthday.'

She wasn't going to admit how much the presence of the lovely Catalina had disturbed her. Beside the Spanish woman's sultry beauty, she had felt pale, wan and insignificant.

'So you made my life hell as a result. Tell me, do you enjoy dragging up the worst moments of our past together? Are you determined to drive me away all over again?'

'On the contrary, I think that you'd better make your mind up, Luis. Either you want to talk this out, or you want to keep quiet. You can't have it both ways. The next few days are going to be difficult enough…'

'The next few days…' Luis echoed, pouncing on the words like a hunter on its prey. 'Does that mean that you're coming with me?'

Had he actually doubted it? Isabelle found that hard to believe. But there was a rough edge to his voice, a disturbing shadow in his eyes that spoke of something very different from the unshakeable self-confidence and arrogant authority he usually displayed.

'Did you give me any choice?' she parried, green eyes flashing defiance as she met that predator's stare head-on. 'I thought it was a royal command and I had no chance of doing anything else.'

Abruptly his expression changed, the shadow in his eyes growing darker, deeper.

'Not a command, *querida*,' he said gruffly. 'A request. One you could grant or refuse as it pleased you. If you come, I want you willing. I want you by my side as my wife…'

'And this will be the real marriage you promised me?'

She could hardly get the words out, they meant so much to her.

'How could it be anything else?' He looked astonished that she should even ask the question. 'You will share my life and my bed. We will be husband and wife in every sense of the word.'

Isabelle's face broke into a wide, brilliant smile of delight, her eyes glowing like emerald fire.

'Then, in that case, I'll come with you,' she said, and when he held out his hand she put hers into it without hesitation.

That smile was in Luis's mind now as he watched her face at the moment that she took in her first sight of his family home. It was one thing knowing that he lived in a castle, quite another being faced by this magnificent hill-top building, parts of which dated back to the sixteenth century.

Built in a warm honey-coloured stone, the castle was approached through gardens of orange groves, oleander and olive trees, beyond which stretched meadows and woodlands. And close by the main courtyard was an aromatic herb garden that scented the air softly.

Luis had stopped the car at the foot of the drive, suggested that they get out and walk from here, sending the chauffeur on ahead with their luggage.

'It's the best way to see the castle,' he told Isabelle. 'And besides, I need to talk to you. There are some things you need to know.'

Isabelle agreed without hesitation. The whole place was so unlike anything she had ever seen in her life that she needed time to adjust, to take in the reality of it. Perhaps if she walked up to it slowly, then she might be able to believe it.

'*This* is where you live?' She looked positively awestruck.

'It's where my parents live. I have my own villa some miles south of here. But my mother and father would never forgive me if I didn't bring you to the family home for their first meeting with you.'

If he was honest, he had never really thought that this day would ever actually happen. Even as he'd knocked on the door of her flat this morning, he had wondered if she would refuse to come with him. He hadn't known if she would welcome him or shut the door right in his face.

And the worrying thing had been how much that had disturbed him. He had found his pulse rate quickening as he'd approached her flat. The hand that he had raised to knock had been unnervingly unsteady.

Seeing her again last night had revived all the hunger, the passion he had once felt for Isabelle, and he had known that he had to have her back in his life, whatever it took. He didn't care if she felt anything for him or not. She was the only woman who had ever made him feel this way, and right now that was enough.

'What was it you wanted to talk to me about?'

From the way his face changed in response to her question, Isabelle knew that she wasn't going to like what he had to say to her.

'Luis—what is it?'

The bronze eyes had darkened swiftly, his jaw tightening, and he stopped walking abruptly, turning to face her.

'I haven't told you everything,' he said sombrely. 'Haven't told you exactly why you're here.'

Isabelle felt as if a cruel hand had suddenly closed over her throat, making it difficult to breathe properly.

'I know why I'm here,' she managed unevenly. 'You asked me to come. To travel to Spain with you—as your wife.'

Why did he hesitate? Why had he suddenly hooded his eyes, shaking his dark head?

'Not exactly,' he said stiffly.

'Not exactly?' Isabelle echoed in confusion. 'Why? What do you mean? What else is there?'

Luis drew in his breath again harshly, raking one hand through the raven darkness of his hair. And that sigh went straight to Isabelle's insides, twisting all her nerves in fearful apprehension.

'Luis! Tell me.'

At last his amber-coloured eyes met hers, fixing her with an intent and unwavering stare.

'I wanted you to come to Spain with me, yes,' he said roughly, clearly reluctantly. 'But not as my wife. I need you to come as my fiancée. To be here as my prospective bride.'

'Your *prospective* bride? What is this?'

Isabelle couldn't believe what she was hearing. She could only stare at him in blank bewilderment, struggling to see his expression clearly in the glare of the sun.

'You have to be joking!'

'It seems clear enough to me.'

Luis moved into the shade of a nearby tree, leaning back against the width of its trunk, and folded his arms across his chest.

'My family don't know I'm married. They don't even know that you exist. If I turn up with you and say that you're my wife, that we've been married for two years already, it will involve us in a lot of complicated, awkward explanations...'

'And why would that matter?'

'My father is ill—seriously ill. He's supposed to avoid all stress or shock.'

'Oh, Luis!'

That drew her shocked green eyes to his carefully shuttered face, one hand going out to touch his arm.

'I'm sorry!'

'*Gracias.*'

It was swift, dismissive. He didn't look as if her sympathy had touched him at all.

'What...?'

'Prostate cancer. He's in remission at the moment, but his time is limited.'

He drew in his breath in a sharp hiss between sharp white teeth.

'I want to make what time he does have happy. That's why you're here. My father wants to see me married—not to find out it's already happened. And Mother has always dreamed of organising a family wedding. Having the service in the cathedral, the reception in the castle. She had hoped to do so for Diegeo, but...'

'I heard about the speedboat accident,' Isabelle inserted quietly when he broke off, his eyes suddenly unfocused. 'That must have been hard on you all.'

'Then you will see why I want to present you to them as my new fiancée.'

'And go through another wedding ceremony? Pretend it's all happening for the first time—lie through my teeth! I think not!'

'That's the way it has to be.'

He was back in aristocratic mode once again. Pure arrogant *conquistador* from his head to his toes.

'The way I want it.'

'The way you want it!' Isabelle echoed bitterly. 'And what do you think is going to happen? That you'll just snap your fingers and I'll jump to do your bidding like some lowly serf you have honoured to notice. I'm a free woman, Luis! I don't let anyone else just run my life.'

'As I've learned to my cost,' he returned sardonically. 'You made sure the word "obey" was omitted from the wedding service, as I recall. And what I *thought* was going to happen was that you were prepared to consider the idea. I thought you'd understand my father's position, the way he feels…'

'I do! Believe me, I do. But even though I understand—and sympathise—that doesn't just mean I'm going to fall in with your plans without question.'

'Would it be so terrible, Isabella?'

'It's that—prospective bride bit. It's a lie.'

'Only a white lie, *querida*. Surely in order to make an ill man happy you can salve your conscience for a little while and play a part. If you can convince a bunch of tourists that there are ghosts walking around York…'

'That's my job! It's what I get paid for.'

'If you want payment—I'll give you anything you want! Think of it as a job. All I ask is that you do your damnedest to be convincing. I want my father and mother to believe we are the happiest couple on earth.'

'I'm not that good an actress.'

'I think you are. I've seen you, remember? I watched you last night. You almost had me convinced that some spirit would come creeping out of the walls of that tower.'

'I was working to a script!'

'Then I will give you a script!'

Reaching out, he took her hand, drew her very close as he looked down into her shadowed green eyes.

'You and I met just a few months ago. I was in England on business. You were at a party I was invited to. We looked into each other's eyes and it was like *un trueno*—a thunderclap. We fell in love in an instant. All we want is to be married. As quickly as possible.'

'Luis…'

She tried to protest, tried to break through the hypnotic spell his voice was weaving around her, but she didn't have the strength. His words were taking her back into the past. Reminding her of how it had once been.

'Think about how it once was with us, Isabella.' Luis bent his proud head, kissed her mouth with heartbreaking softness. 'It wasn't so very long ago. Surely you can remember that?'

How could she forget it? It was etched into her memories, branded on her heart. It had been all she had ever dreamed of. And now it was what she wanted back most in all the world.

And when he looked at her like that, when the husky, enticing tones of his softly accented voice pleaded with her to do as he asked, she was helpless, soft as wax in his hands.

'All—all right, I'll…' she began shakily, but Luis didn't give her a chance to complete her sentence. Lacing his fingers in hers, he squeezed her hand tight.

'It's not so very far from the truth,' he told her, leading her up the remainder of the drive and into the stone-flagged courtyard of the castle.

But almost immediately it was as if the shadows cast by the high walls had fallen over Isabelle's heart. Her steps slowed, coming to a complete halt as she looked up at the huge, carved oak door.

'What is it?'

'I don't think I can.'

'*Por Dios*, why the hell not? You've come this far, you can't back out now.'

'But I don't think I can go through with it.'

'Of course you can.'

He dismissed her fears with an arrogant little flick of his hand.

'But if you want a little help…'

Before she knew what was coming, he had reached out and caught hold of her arm. Swinging her round, he brought her up close to him, held tight against the hard wall of his chest.

'This should do it,' he muttered roughly as his head came down, his mouth taking hers hard and fast, crushing her lips underneath his.

The world seemed to swing around her, her thoughts filling with a buzzing haze. The warmth of the sun was as nothing when compared to the heat that was flooding her body, making her heart pound fiercely, setting her blood throbbing in her veins.

She responded instinctively, urgent hands clutching at his powerful shoulders, fingers digging into the hard muscle underneath the fine cotton of his navy shirt. Her mouth opened under his, allowing, and hungrily responding to the tantalising dance of provocation of his tongue. Her pliant body arched towards his, glorying in the feeling of his male strength against her own, and electric thrill sparking in every nerve as she felt the heated pressure of his erection against the softness of her pelvis. Hard hands cupped her buttocks, pressing her even closer.

When Luis finally released her, she was breathing hard and unevenly. Her scalp tingled where his hands had twisted in her hair, and she knew that her face was flushed, her eyes over-bright as if she had a fever.

Which she did, she admitted to herself. Luis was like a fever in her blood, a fatal addiction. She would never be free of him, and, if the truth was told, she never wanted to be. He was all she had ever dreamed of in a man.

'There…'

Luis's voice was rich with dark satisfaction, a tiger's purr of pleasure.

'Now you look like a newly engaged fiancée. A woman hopelessly in love with the man she has agreed to marry.'

Of course she did, Isabelle admitted to herself. She looked that way because she really was that woman. There was no point in trying to deny it, or hide it from herself any longer.

The one thing and the one alone that had brought her here was the fact that her love for Luis had never died. The flame of it still burned deep inside her heart, unwavering and unquenchable, in spite of all their years apart.

'And, Isabella—'

But whatever Luis had been about to say went unfinished. His words were interrupted by the sound of footsteps behind the heavy door, the buzz of puzzled Spanish reaching them vaguely through the solid wood.

'My family,' he said abruptly. 'They heard the car and they've grown tired of waiting so they've come looking for us. Ready?'

Isabelle could only shake her head, a terrible sense of apprehension freezing her tongue and making her breath catch in her throat.

'There's no need to look like that.' Luis actually sounded as if he understood, the gentleness in his voice knocking her right off balance. 'They won't bite.'

'But what if they don't like me?'

Her voice shook with the strain of controlling her real fears. She had come here in the hope of reviving what she and Luis had once had, of convincing him that he had been wrong to believe she could ever be unfaithful to him. But what if he never changed his mind? What if he never ever loved her again?

'How could they not like you?' he asked now. 'All they ask for is that you make me happy. And you will.'

'I will? How—?'

But she couldn't finish the question because at that moment the door was pulled open and a tall, black-haired woman appeared, her arms outstretched in welcome.

'Luis, welcome home. And this—is this lovely young woman your fiancée?'

'Sí Mama.'

Luis moved forwards, one strong arm snaking round Isabelle's waist, taking her with him.

'Isabella, come and meet my mother...'

Desperate to hide her nervousness, Isabelle switched on a smile that she prayed looked genuine. But it faltered, almost disappearing as Luis bent his dark head until his mouth was close to her ear.

'You know only too well how to make me happy, *mi angel*,' he whispered, warm breath feathering over her skin. 'Just as I know exactly how to please you. And if you're good, I'll prove it to you tonight.'

CHAPTER FIVE

ISABELLE leaned her arms on the wide stone sill of the castle's arched windows and stared out at the darkened landscape, a low despondent sigh escaping her. She felt lost and isolated, a crazy, inexplicable feeling in a place full of people, but the truth was that she had never known loneliness like it.

She didn't know who she was or where she belonged any more. She was Luis's wife and yet here, amongst his family, she was only his fiancée. The *duque* and *duquesa* had welcomed her into their home, treated her like an honoured guest, but she knew that her presence here was just a pretence, that she was deceiving them by pretending to be something she was not. And Luis...

The sigh deepened. The truth was that she just didn't really know how Luis saw her.

A soft sound of a knock at the door startled her, bringing her head up sharply.

'Who is it?'

'Your fiancé of course.' Even through the thickness of the door, the irony in Luis's tone was clear. 'Were you expecting someone else?'

'I wasn't expecting anyone,' Isabelle protested as she wrenched open the door. 'Least of all you. What are you doing here?'

'I'm performing my duties as your host,' he drawled sardonically, black straight brows lifting in disapproval at her tone. 'I came to see if you were comfortable and your room was okay.'

She couldn't look him in the face, every heightened sense was too aware of him for that. He was still wearing the trousers of the elegant silver grey silk suit he had changed into for dinner, but he had discarded the jacket somewhere. The fine linen of his white shirt clung softly to the firm lines of his torso, emphasising the width of chest and broad straight shoulders. He had tugged his tie loose at the neck, unfastening a couple of buttons, and the immaculate colour seemed to glow vividly against the smooth tanned skin of his throat.

'Luis, you've seen my flat. You know that compared to that this…' her gesture took in the elegantly furnished room with a genuine four-poster bed, thick rose-coloured carpet and curtains '…is total luxury. I couldn't be more comfortable.'

'You're quite sure you have everything you need.'

'I'm perfectly fine! You don't even have to ask that! Goodnight.'

To emphasise the point, she tried to shut the door in his face, only to find the movement prevented by the swift insertion of one elegantly booted foot into the open space.

'I also thought you might like a nightcap.'

He lifted a hand to display a bottle of red wine and two glasses hooked between his fingers.

'Something to relax you.'

'I think not.'

'It's from our own vineyards,' he continued imperturbably, obviously unconcerned by her unwelcoming tone. 'I think you'd enjoy it.'

'And what would your parents think to that?'

Luis affected a pretence of not understanding, widening his eyes in a display of innocence.

'Think to what, *querida*?'

'To your being here, alone, with me at this time of night. Wouldn't they think—?'

'They wouldn't expect anything else,' Luis inserted smoothly, flooring her completely. 'We are, after all, man and wife.'

'But your parents don't know that!'

'They know that we are engaged, and they are modern minded enough to know that very few couples actually wait until they've exchanged vows before they share a bed together.'

'But all the same…'

Her grip on the door had loosened a little, her concentration wavering. Luis took full advantage of the situation by pushing it wider and slipping in through the open space. Strolling across the room, he deposited the bottle and glasses on the bedside table, pulled a corkscrew from his pocket and set about stripping the foil from the bottle with swift efficiency.

'My parents, *amada*, would be very surprised, not to say concerned, if we didn't want to spend some time alone together, particularly at this new and very special stage in our relationship.'

He didn't look her in the eyes as he spoke, his attention apparently on opening the bottle, extracting the cork as smoothly and skilfully as possible.

'They believe we have just become engaged. That we are madly in love with each other.'

'And we both know that that couldn't be further from the truth!' Uncertainty and tension pushed the words from her mouth.

Luis's busy hands stilled suddenly, his whole body freezing into immobility in a way that made her heart clench sharply. But a moment later he had returned to his task, apparently focusing only on that and nothing else.

'Is that a fact?' he drawled at last, his words punctuated by the faint pop as the cork finally slid from the bottle.

Isabelle's heart, which had started to relax, tightened up again, more fearfully this time, as she tried to interpret just what his tone of voice might mean.

'Here, taste this.'

Luis was pleased with his tone, the smoothness of his voice. He hadn't missed a beat, covering his reaction to that ill-timed comment.

So what had he expected? That she would have come right out with a declaration of love? He'd have to be dreaming for that to happen. And he'd never thought of himself as a dreamer. All his life he'd lived on purely pragmatic terms— except once, when he'd fallen hopelessly and totally in love with this woman. Insanely in love, because he'd never fully recovered his wits since.

There, he'd admitted it to himself at last. Ever since that moment in York when he'd seen her coming towards him, dressed in that spectacular gown, he'd known he wasn't over her. The sensation of being kicked in the gut he could explain away as a purely physical reaction—though his thoughts had been at the opposite extreme to *pure*. But it was the absurd and impossible lifting of his heart that had told him he was in deep trouble.

'It's delicious.'

Isabelle's voice seemed to come from a long distance away, forcing him to drag his attention back to the moment.

'I thought you'd like it.'

Did she know how the rich ruby colour of the wine had stained her mouth, emphasising the soft fullness of her lower lip? The memory of how sweet that mouth had tasted, how it had opened invitingly under his kiss, instantly triggered his body's response so that he had to swing away to stare out of the window until he could get himself back under control.

But there was no escape. Even as he stared out at the darkened sky, he could still see her slender, feminine body in the pretty floral-print dress reflected in the glass before him.

'And perhaps it might relax me. I was too nervous to drink very much at dinner.'

'Or eat very much.'

He'd hardly touched his food himself, moving it about on his plate in a pretence at interest in it. But all his attention had been focused on the woman sitting opposite, her blonde hair gleaming in the flickering light of the candles, her soft voice answering his parents' questions with careful politeness.

'You were every bit as bad as me.'

He hadn't expected that and it brought him swinging round in shock, amber eyes flying straight to her face.

'You noticed?'

'Oh, I noticed. You messed about, but put very little in your mouth.'

Her laugh was slightly shaky, no real warmth in it.

'I don't know what your parents must have thought of the

two of us. I just hope they don't think there was something wrong with the food and sack the cook.'

'Don't worry, the chef's job is safe. They'll think we're both so completely lovesick that we've lost our appetites. And they'll expect you to have been nervous, so they'll understand.'

'I wasn't nervous! I never felt unsure with your mother and father. They couldn't have been kinder and they made me feel right at home from the start. That was the problem.'

'What problem?'

'Isn't it obvious? They're lovely people; I don't like deceiving them. In fact, now that I've met them, I hate it even more.'

'Is this your way of trying to say you want out of this?'

Luis moved forward, picked up his own drink, trying to look as if the answer to his question didn't matter a damn to him.

'Not at all. If anything, now that I've met your father, I want to go through with it even more. He's a lovely person, I took to him straight away and I'm so sorry that he's ill.'

'He likes you too.'

'And that's what makes this pretence so difficult. I just wish we could do this without deceiving him—and without all the fuss.'

The sudden shake in her voice, the way she sipped hastily at her drink, gave her away.

'You're scared?'

Her eyes looked like dark green ponds, deep and shadowed, as she glanced up at him.

'Aren't you? No, I suppose not. You must be used to all this—a wedding in the cathedral, pictures for the press. Do we really have to have a reception for all the village?'

'It isn't what I thought was ahead of me, remember. I always thought this would be Diego's role in life. That as the eldest son and heir, he'd be the one going through the ceremonial wedding. But, yes, I'm afraid we do have to put up with it. They'll expect it. It comes with the territory—marrying into a branch of the royal family, however small and obscure. Though in our case, it's more like a twig.'

The tiny, half-hearted smile that flashed on and off her face left him in little doubt how she was feeling. Inwardly he cursed his mother's over-enthusiasm for the wedding plans that had had her launching into them as soon as they had sat down for dinner. But then Dona Elvira had been looking forward to this moment for years. And she had no idea of the secret undercurrents running through the situation. The delicious cold gazpacho soup had barely been served before she had started a discussion on dresses and flowers and bridesmaids.

'Hey, it's not that bad.'

'Isn't it?'

She swung away from him, headed for the small settee beside the huge stone fireplace. The fact that she sat staring fixedly into the empty hearth told its own story, and Luis saw that her teeth were worrying at her bottom lip.

'Isabella—don't.'

He came to sit beside her, lifted an arm to put it round her shoulders, then changed his mind. A moment later he changed it back again and let his arm fall, his hand closing over the fine bones of her arm.

'You'll be fine. And I'll be there with you.'

That brought her head round sharply, her expression startled.

'Will you?'

'Where the hell else would I be? After all, it's my wedding too. And perhaps this will help make you feel better.'

Isabelle could only stare numbly as Luis pulled a box from his pocket and took out a spectacular diamond ring. She didn't resist as he took her hand and pushed the ring onto the appropriate finger where it fitted perfectly.

'How—how did you know my size?'

His mouth took on a cynical twist.

'I remembered it. I have bought you a ring before, remember?'

How could she forget when the ring in question hung on a

slender chain around her neck, nestling safe inside an identical but much larger one. The ring she had placed on his finger on their wedding day. The ring he had thrown at her in such a fury on the day he had walked out of her life.

'I always promised you a proper engagement ring. We were in such a hurry to get married that you never had one before.'

'And this is very definitely a *proper* engagement ring.'

And then, when she was totally emotionally unready to do so, she recalled his comment at the door of the castle. 'You know only too well how to make me happy, *mi angel*,' he had said. 'And if you're good, I'll prove it to you tonight.' And with a sickening lurch of her heart she knew why he was here.

'So when do I start reimbursing you for this? Because I presume you expect me to earn it with some sort of payment in kind.'

Her question earned her a glare of angry reproof, one that made her shift uncomfortably on the brocade couch.

'It comes with no conditions attached,' he growled angrily. 'I gave it to you because my parents would know something was amiss if I didn't. They would expect my fiancée to be wearing a ring—I have provided one. Our story would not ring true otherwise.'

It was controlled, so emotionless that it stabbed at her vulnerable heart. It was impossible not to contrast his behaviour now with the ardent, impulsive proposal of marriage he had made just over two years before.

'But our story isn't true, is it, Luis? I don't see why we can't just tell them—'

The look on his face, the dark anger that blazed in his eyes, stopped her dead.

'Tell them what, *mi angel*? Do you really want me to explain to my parents why we split up in the first place? Shall I tell them that you were found in bed with another man only a few weeks after we were married?'

'I told you—!'

'I know what you told me, but forgive me...' Luis laced the words with an acid that turned them into the exact opposite of any genuine attempt at an apology '...I prefer to believe the evidence of my own eyes.'

'The evidence you were supposed to believe! It was a set-up!'

Luis's dark frown dried her mouth, stilled her impetuous tongue.

'Was Rob Michaels in your bed?' he questioned harshly, every bit the counsel for the prosecution.

'Yes.'

It was barely a whisper but there was nothing she could say except the truth. She *had* woken up to find Rob in her bed, but she had had no idea how he had got there. Her memory of the night before had been decidedly hazy as the result of a very bad cold and some medication she had taken. And before she had had a chance to demand to know what he'd been doing there, the whole world had blown up in her face.

She shuddered miserably as her mind replayed snatches from that terrible night. The sound of a key in the lock. The door swinging open. The light snapping on.

And there, framed in the doorway, with a face as black as a thundercloud, bronze eyes molten in fury—Luis. Her husband.

'And why is lying to my parents so very hard? After all, you have lied to me about much more important things.'

'I never...'

Her face was pale, her green eyes huge above colourless cheeks. He had the fight of his life with himself not to take her in his arms and tell her it was all right, that it didn't matter.

He forced himself to continue.

'Did you not swear to me that you loved me more than life itself? That you could never imagine yourself with anyone else, loving anyone else...'

His voice lowered, became a deadly, vindictive hiss.

'Sleeping with anyone else.'

It was crueller than any slap in the face. All the more so because it had been delivered in such a quiet, controlled voice. But then she looked into his eyes and to her shock it was not anger or cruelty that she saw there, but the soul-deep pain of betrayal.

'I've *told* you...'

'I know what you've told me. But until you can come up with something better than, "It was a set-up," I'm sorry, but I cannot believe you.'

The last thing he sounded was sorry, Isabelle reflected miserably. Instead his tone was icily cold, laced with a bitter control she couldn't see her way past. Unable to bear the way that the same dark feeling showed in his gaze, she pressed her hands to her face for a moment, covering her own eyes with them.

'I had a heavy cold,' she said from behind her concealing fingers, putting all the conviction she could muster into the words, willing him to believe them. 'Catalina gave me something for it and I went to bed early. The next thing I knew was when I woke up when you came into the room.'

'A room that was locked from the inside. I had to go down to Reception and get the master key.'

'Rob must have locked it.'

'And how did he get inside in the first place?'

'I don't know!'

Isabelle snatched her hands away from her face, flinging them out in a wild gesture to emphasise her words.

'I *don't know*.'

It wasn't enough. She could read it in his dark, shuttered face, the way his eyes were hooded under half-closed lids. He didn't believe her. And really, deep down, she knew she couldn't blame him.

Would *she* have believed *him* if the positions had been reversed? If she had been the one coming home late from a long trip to London to see her brother and she had walked in on Luis, naked, in bed with someone else—with Catalina, for example. Would he have been able to convince her that it was all perfectly innocent? That he had fallen asleep alone and woken up to find the other woman in his bed?

It sounded impossible and totally unbelievable. And she knew that she would have reacted just as he had done. That she would have walked away in a black fury of pain and betrayal and never looked back.

'Luis, we'd had a row…'

'I know what had happened. You do not have to remind me. We argued and so—so what? You punished me by sleeping with the first man who asked?'

'You can't believe that!'

No, Luis admitted privately, she was right, damn it! He couldn't believe it. He hadn't then and he couldn't now. If anyone had asked him, he would have sworn on his life that Isabelle loved him. That she would always be faithful. That was why finding her with Michaels had hit him so hard that he had thought he would go crazy, do something totally unforgivable, if he hadn't got out of there at once.

'It was what you threatened to do,' he said dully. 'And Rob Michaels had been sniffing around you for weeks.'

Isabelle winced away from his words, and the pain she could hear behind them, wishing she could deny the truth, but knowing that she could not.

'It was an empty threat. I never meant it. Certainly not like that. I was angry—hurt. It was my birthday, Luis.'

Her tone pleaded for understanding.

'My first birthday with you and you spent it away from me.'

'I had no choice; you knew that. My father was only in London for that day. I had to see him to try to bridge some of the distance that had come between us. I had no other opportunity.'

She understood that now, Isabelle admitted to herself, but then, barely twenty-one, and still in the throes of the first obsessive, possessive love for her new husband, she had been unwilling to share him with anyone, even his family. She had insisted he stay with her—or at least take her with him. And when he had refused she had lost her temper.

'All right, go!' she had flung at him, blind to the danger signs of his tightly set mouth, the tension in his hard jaw, the muscle that had flickered just above it. 'Go if you want, and leave me on my own! But don't expect me to stay on my own!

If you won't be with me on my birthday, I'll find someone else who will.'

It had been a hollow threat, bad-tempered, childish and petulant, and she had never dreamed that it might rebound on her so appallingly, until it had been too late.

'I can see that now, Luis,' she admitted miserably. 'And I was very stupid, very selfish—but that's all I was. Please don't hate me for being stupid.'

'I don't.'

He didn't hate her.

Dios, didn't she know that he could never *hate* her? That was the reason she could get to him so badly. The reason why he'd had to come to England when he'd got that letter. He'd tried to convince himself that he never wanted to see her again, but the truth was that he had never felt anything so terrible as the fear that he might lose her for good. And he'd endured that fear twice now.

'Why do you think you are here? I forgave you—'

'Forgave!'

Isabelle couldn't believe what she was hearing and her distress was a savage wound in her heart as she faced the way her hopes had been lifted, only to be dashed right down in the next second. She could hardly bear to look into his face, to see the way he had stiffened, the golden eyes narrowing, his jaw setting hard and tight.

How could he have taken her so close to the future she had dreamed of and then snatched it away again? She felt as if she had been given a glimpse of heaven, only to have the door slammed right in her face.

'I didn't want *forgiveness* for something I didn't do! I wanted trust! The sort of trust that doesn't need proof—that believes in me completely and totally. And if you can't give me that, then our marriage has no future and we might just as well forget the whole thing!'

That got through to him. It slashed straight through everything else he had been feeling, stabbed straight to the heart. And in that moment he knew that, two years before, he had made the worst, most appalling mistake of his life.

There had always been something he had kept coming back to, something he hadn't been able to quite put his finger on, and it had disturbed him, nagged at him throughout the past two years. Now he knew he wouldn't be able to rest until he'd cleared the whole matter up. And if he had been wrong, then he'd spend the rest of his life making it up to Isabelle.

'I don't want to forget it,' he muttered harshly.

Isabelle didn't know how to take that.

'Oh, Luis, *mi marido, mi amor…*'

'No!'

He couldn't bear those words. Not now. Not when he feared that he had wronged her so badly.

Pushing himself to his feet, he swung halfway across the room, needing to put a physical distance between them that matched the emotional one he had let grow because of his stupid hurt pride.

'Don't call me that. Not now.'

Isabelle knew her mistake as soon as the words had left her lips, and desperately, hopelessly, wished them back, knowing there was no chance of salvation.

Beside her she had felt Luis's hard length tense, freezing in shock, and then, agonisingly, the immediate, inevitable swift withdrawal, the movement away that spelled out his rejection, tearing her heart in two.

'Luis, *mi marido, mi amor…*' The first few words of Spanish he had taught her. The most important words, he had said. If she never learned any other phrases, then these would do. They would say all she ever needed to say to keep him happy.

But one night she had used those words and known they would never have the same effect again. That even if she handed her heart to him at the same time, he would never, ever believe that she loved him.

They had been the last words she had shouted after him on that dreadful night when he had arrived back unexpectedly and found her and Rob, in bed together. She had tried to explain but he had turned from her as he was doing now, his eyes dark with rejection. And so she had screamed the only words she had thought might bring him back.

But they had had as little effect as they were having now. His face had closed up, steel shutters seeming to slam shut behind his eyes, cutting him off from her completely. And he had walked out of her life—for good, it had seemed.

The words swung round and round in Luis's head, gaining a new and terrible bitterness with every repetition.

My husband, my love... Once he had longed to hear her say them as often as she could. He would have sworn that he would never grow tired of them. That he could never hear anything that would have made him happier.

Until one bitter dawn when he had heard her shout them after him down a long, shadowy hotel corridor as he'd walked away from the terrible sight of her and her lover in bed together.

He hadn't been able to bear to stay a second longer then. He had had to get away—fast—just as he had to now. If he stayed, then he would surely give himself away completely, by letting her know just how he was feeling. And the truth was that he was such a mess, such a knot of tangled emotions deep inside, that he didn't know what to say to her.

'L-Luis...' Isabelle tried, but her voice failed her completely, shrivelling into nothing as he turned back to her and she saw the tightness of every muscle in his face, the blank, opaque eyes.

'Perdón,' he said stiffly. 'Forgive me, but I cannot...'

My husband, my love. But if he had loved her enough he would have stayed. He would have listened. He would have trusted.

He had done no such thing. He had failed her. And now he would have to live with his conscience for having wronged her so badly.

'You were right, Isabella,' he went on harshly. 'Perhaps we should forget the whole thing. I will not trouble you again.'

Not until he could prove to her that he believed in her the way she needed him to.

'But, Luis…' Isabelle began, but she was speaking to empty air.

Without even another glance in her direction, Luis had marched from the room and she could only stare in silent desperation as the door swung to behind him.

'Forgive me, but I cannot…' His cold, stiff words seemed to hang in the air, freezing, like the cruel hand that gripped her heart.

'I cannot…' What? If he could never forget what had happened, then what possible hope of a future was there?

CHAPTER SIX

'ALL alone, my dear?'

'What?'

Isabelle looked up in surprise, struggling to drag herself into the present as Luis's father came towards her along the stone-flagged terrace.

'Is that son of mine neglecting you?'

'He—he had business to attend to. Something about one of the vineyards.'

It was an excuse that would do as well as any other, she told herself. It was the one Luis had used to explain his absences at first.

But lately he had stopped doing even that. He had just headed out at the start of the day, some mornings even before she was awake, and he was more often than not very late back.

'The vineyards can take care of themselves.' The duke frowned into the sun. 'Luis should be here.'

'He will be,' Isabelle put in hastily, hoping she sounded more confident than she actually felt. 'I think he just wants to make sure that everything is in order before we leave on our honeymoon.'

A honeymoon that was now not so far away. The days since she had come to Spain had flashed by so fast that she could hardly believe she had been here a month or more now. Every day had been taken up with some sort of planning or preparation for the wedding so that she had barely had time to think.

And if she was honest, she'd been grateful for the endless round of fittings, consultations, coffee mornings, visits to relatives that had filled her time and taken her away from Luis's disturbing absences and his even more disturbing presence in the brief times he had actually spent in the castle.

'How are you feeling today?'

157

Don Alfonso always looked pale, and his tall frame hadn't an ounce of spare flesh on it. But the bronze eyes that were so like his son's were bright and alert these days, his energy belying his state of health.

'I feel fine,' he assured her now, a smile lighting up his face. 'So I was wondering if you'd like that history lesson now.'

'The tour of the gallery?' Isabelle was already on her feet. 'I'd love to.'

It was something that she and the duke had discussed some days before. From the first, Isabelle had been fascinated by the long gallery of portraits of the de Silva family, ancestors of Luis, long-ago dukes and duchesses, dating right back to the time of the Spanish Inquisition. She had wanted to learn more about them, but the time had never been quite right.

The afternoon passed in total absorption. As Don Alfonso had said, this was a history lesson, but the characters involved were his family. Luis's family. Her family by marriage now. And for the first time she had a real sense of how Luis must feel, with the weight of all that lineage behind him.

'It must be amazing to know that you have ancestors who were brothers or sisters of kings,' she said when a couple of hours later they made their way back down the long, sweeping stone staircase into the main hall again.

'It's an honour and a responsibility,' the duke added sombrely. 'Our family has great wealth but we also owe a great deal to our heritage and should never treat it lightly.'

'Living here must make you feel like that. Knowing that this castle has been in the family for so many hundreds of years.'

'And it will be into the future too. That has always been my dream. That is why in our family marriage and children are so important. When Diego died, I thought...'

He caught himself up, shaking his head, the golden eyes dimmed for a moment, but then he reached for Isabelle's hand and squeezed it gently.

'But your marriage to Luis will ensure that our line will go on. Your children will inherit the dukedom. Yours and Luis's.'

The words caught Isabelle on the raw, stirring uncomfortable memories of yet another reason for her distress over the past weeks. Even the blazing passion that had flared between herself and Luis on that first night in York seemed to have died. He hadn't even come to her room, hadn't shared her bed since they had arrived.

There was a discreet cough behind them, a maid trying to get their attention.

'Don Alfonso… You have a visitor. Señorita del Bosque.'

'Catalina? I thought she was in America.'

Something in the way the older man said the name, his expression as he looked towards the room the maid had indicated, betrayed the way he was feeling. He would never admit to being tired, but clearly he had had enough.

'Shall I see what she wants?' Isabelle suggested. 'I met Catalina once—back in England. I'll talk to her if you like.'

Her reward was another of those charming, warm smiles that twisted in her heart with the memories they revived. Memories of the days when she had first met Luis. When his smile had been so swift and so delightful, so easily won.

'If you wouldn't mind, my dear. I would appreciate it.'

'Why are you sitting here in the dark?'

Luis's voice coincided with the snapping on of the light, startling Isabelle so that she jumped nervously, wide green eyes turning to where he stood in the doorway.

'I—I was thinking.'

She looked distant, Luis thought, as if her mind was somewhere else. And there was something in the way she sat, a lack of colour in her cheeks, the unsmiling mouth, that made him tense instinctively. He could almost scent trouble in the air but he had no idea where it came from.

'Thinking about what?'

'The wedding.'

It was the easy answer because she wasn't yet ready to tell him the truth. What she had thought would simply be a social chat with Catalina had turned into something that had rocked her whole world. Something she didn't yet know how to handle. For one thing, she needed to be sure, to know that it was actually fact. And to do that, she had to test the water first.

'Oh, that.'

He had thought it would be more. The realisation that that was all it was should have relaxed him, but there was still something about the atmosphere in the room that did nothing to ease his unsettled frame of mind.

'So, what's been on your busy schedule today?'

Luis strolled into the room and settled himself in the chair opposite Isabelle, leaning back tiredly.

'Did you have another fitting for the wedding dress of the year? Or perhaps an important meeting to decide about the colour of flowers?'

'Actually, today I didn't have anything planned. Most things are just about in hand.'

Isabelle was frankly surprised by the bite in Luis's voice. Anyone would have thought that he was—*jealous* was the word that sprang to mind. But that couldn't possibly be true.

'Good. Then perhaps in that case you might like to consider having lunch with me tomorrow? Maybe even spending the day together?'

'Well—yes—if that's what you want.'

If his mood had surprised her, then this invitation rocked her even more. It broke into the routine they had established. The routine that she had thought worked well. The routine that she believed was the way Luis wanted to run things.

After lying awake late into the long, lonely hours before dawn on her first night in the castle, after Luis had walked out on her, she had finally come to a decision. There was only one way that she could handle this situation. One way that she could behave so that she could get through the days being the wife Luis wanted and still keep any sort of hold on her sanity and her feelings.

She was going to have to pretend. She was going to have to put on the act of her life and draw on every last ounce of her dramatic ability and training if she was to be in the least bit convincing.

She would have to play the newly engaged fiancée, still

starry-eyed in the first throes of love. The prospective bride who had every happiness to look forward to and who was planning the wedding of her dreams with heartfelt delight, while all the time she knew that the man she loved felt nothing for her but the dark physical passion that had ensnared both of them on the night he had come to find her in York.

And she had thought that she might just manage that. Or at least she had done, until today.

Until Catalina had appeared and let her in on a couple of bitterly painful truths.

'It isn't a matter of what I want,' Luis growled. 'More that my parents are hardly going to believe we're hopelessly in love with each other if we rarely spend as much as half an hour in each other's company except at mealtimes.'

'You're the one who's always out—"on business",' Isabelle pointed out. 'And there's a lot to do to plan a wedding—especially the sort of wedding your mother has in mind.'

'It has seemed to be the only thing you think about.'

It had been impossible to get near her, in fact, Luis thought. Looking back over the past three weeks, it seemed she had been almost constantly occupied, dashing here to choose table decorations, or there to look at flowers.

She had been perfectly polite and pleasant, but somehow ethereal. Being with her had been like trying to grab hold of a soap bubble. Just when he thought he had it in his hands it would burst and disintegrate into nothing.

They barely spoke at all. At least not about anything important. And because he had vowed that he wouldn't touch her until he believed he had the right, all other forms of communication were closed to them too.

'Your mother wants everything to be perfect.'

'I know.'

Luis's sigh was low, despondent, and his bronze eyes clouded as he stared at the floor.

'She's putting her heart and soul into this wedding because it will be the only one,' he said, unknowingly reviving memories of the way the duke had spoken earlier. 'She always dreamed of planning Diego's wedding too.'

'That must be hard for all of you.'

Something had put an edge into her voice, drawing his frowning gaze to her face, but she simply returned his look with a blank one of her own as she continued.

'I know how you felt about your brother. It must have been a terrible day for you all when he died.'

'I thought my father would never recover.'

Luis raked his free hand through the black silk of his hair, the shiny black strands catching the sunlight as they fell back over his high forehead.

'Since then I've felt I've had to be both sons for him.'

'He's looked better recently. Brighter and happier.'

'He sees the hope of a future and that gives him something to keep going for. You've done that for him.'

'Not just me—it's both of us together. And the wedding.'

She flexed shoulders that were tight with tension and closed her eyes briefly against the sting of tears. She would have given the world not to believe what Catalina had told her, but with every word that Luis spoke the dread grew darker, her fears stronger that the Spanish woman had spoken nothing but the truth.

'You're not enjoying it?' Luis had misinterpreted the reasons for her low spirits. 'I would have thought that for any woman the chance to have a wedding dress specially designed by a Paris couturier, a wedding in a cathedral, would be like a dream come true.'

The dream come true, Isabelle reflected sadly, would be to know that the man she was marrying loved her as much as she loved him. With that, the simplest, most inexpensive wedding would be perfect, and without it all the money in the world couldn't provide compensation for what was missing.

'For some people, perhaps,' she said slowly, keeping her eyes lowered so as not to have to look into his darkly devastating face. 'But if you want to know the truth, then I much preferred our first wedding in that little chapel in York.'

'Walking to the church in the rain?' Frank disbelief rang in

Luis's voice, stilling the restless movement of Isabelle's hand on the arm of her chair.

'It was only a little shower. Not even a drizzle really.'

And she had been so happy that she hadn't noticed the weather at all. The sky might have been dull and grey but in her heart there had been nothing but sunshine and her feet had felt as if they weren't touching the ground, as if she were floating down the damp pavements towards her destiny.

'And I was so thrilled when I found that dress in a boutique sale. What?' she asked in some surprise when his head came up, bronze eyes fixed on her face.

'I was just remembering how wonderful you looked in it,' Luis told her, his voice rough as if it came from a painfully dry throat. 'So beautiful, so fresh and innocent.'

Even when he had thought he hated her, he had never been able to erase from his mind the memory of that moment when he had turned and seen her walking down the aisle of the tiny chapel, wearing the simple white cotton dress, carrying a single rose by way of a bouquet. Her golden hair had gleamed in a soft halo around her glowing face, her lips had been curved into a smile of pure delight, and her eyes had never looked so brilliant, shining a wonderful, emerald green.

'Your Paris designer is going to have to work hard to do any better.'

'I don't think he'll do better—it'll just be different. In the same way that this reception for five hundred will be so different from...'

'From the picnic by the river?' Luis supplied when, overcome by memory, she couldn't supply the words. 'That was something else.'

'At—at least the sun had come out by then.'

The darkness in his eyes was tying her nerves into tight, painful knots. Looking into his handsome face now, she was suddenly taken back to that day, remembering the happiness, the hope for the future, she had felt then.

'I couldn't believe my luck,' Luis went on, his voice growing even deeper on each word. 'I kept looking across at you and thinking— She's my wife. That's *my wife*.'

Abruptly his expression changed, a deep frown bringing his black brows together.

'Should I have made it different for you, Isabella? Should I have swallowed my pride, forgotten the arguments I'd had with my father and brought you here, married you...'

'In a wedding like the one we're having now? Do you want the truth, Luis?'

The memory of Catalina's words that afternoon came back to haunt her, stiffening her pride and tightening her voice.

'Because if you do, then the answer is no. I wouldn't have wanted it any other way. I loved you so much then. Couldn't have been happier... This wedding can never be the same. And neither can our marriage.'

'Okay, maybe we can never go back to that innocent, idyllic time, but perhaps we can find something to put in its place.'

'What sort of something?'

'Well...'

Abruptly Luis caught himself up, a prey to a sensation of doubt, as cold and sneaking as if a cloud had just passed in front of the sun.

I loved you, she had said. Not I *love* you. He wanted to tell her everything that was in his heart. Let her know that the past didn't matter—that all that mattered was her and the way he felt about her. But if he did—and she didn't feel the same way...

'Something' of that feeling was all she wanted back. Not the whole, heartfelt loving that had once been the most essential part of his life.

Better not to rush things. Better to take it one step at a time. To offer only a part of what he was feeling and then see where that took them. At least then, if she couldn't give him the same love back, he wouldn't risk the pain of loss all over again. It had taken him two long years to get over that sensation, the feeling that she hadn't loved him as he had loved her. He didn't think he could ever recover from it a second time.

So he caught back the impulsive declaration he had been about to make, stamping down on the protestations of love and belief in her, and instead substituted a careful, controlled explanation of the future they might have.

'We could have a future together—children…'

Her reaction was not at all as he had anticipated.

'Children? You want children?'

Any hope she'd had that she'd been wrong, that Catalina had lied, died as soon as she looked into his face. Suddenly too much on edge to stay still, she got to her feet, pacing restlessly about the room.

'Of course I want children. I told you—I want a proper marriage and everything that it entails.'

'Your father wants you to have children too. I get the impression that he'd like us to have them as soon as possible.'

Luis nodded swift agreement.

'I think it's the most important thing in the world to him.'

Abruptly Luis got to his feet, moving to stare out of the huge arched window through which the vast gardens of the castle could just be seen in the moonlight. His head was bent slightly, his shoulders hunched, his hands pushed deep into the pockets of his trousers.

'I really believe that he is holding on because of his dream of grandchildren. That he is fighting harder because he wants to stay alive for that.'

There, it was out. He had never thought that he would ever tell anyone the truth of his beliefs. But he had not been able to hold the words back. Somehow being with Isabelle again had broken into the reticence that was so much a part of his relationship with his parents. To her he had been able to say the things he had never been able to say to his mother or anyone else.

'You could be right.'

Her voice behind him was surprisingly soft. He turned slowly back to face her.

'A positive attitude seems to be a very strong weapon in the fight against such illnesses.'

'You sound as if you know about such things.'

'My grandmother—the one who brought me up after my parents were killed in that motorway pile-up—had cancer. She refused to give in to it. Believe me, I know what you're going through.'

'Then you'll see why it matters to me too. He started talking about my getting married as soon as he knew I would be his heir. His one wish is to see the future of the de Silva dynasty secure—the prospect of grandchildren to inherit the dukedom when he is gone. That's why Diego's death hit my father hardest of all. He had been grooming my brother as his successor. Now he had to start all over again.'

He didn't have to elaborate on what had put that note into his voice. Isabelle remembered only too well how he had told her of the way his father, Duke Alfonso, had always favoured his elder son. As an adolescent and a young man, Luis had rebelled against both this and the formal dignity of his position. That was why he had been in England, taking any unskilled job he could, in the first place.

Isabelle had never dreamed that the charming drifter with the melting eyes and equally liquid accent, who worked as a waiter in a wine bar, was actually a member of one of the noble houses of Spain, only a step away from the royal family. By the time he'd told her, she had already fallen totally in love with him.

'So, naturally, you wanted to please him.'

A quick, abrupt inclination of his head indicated agreement.

'And make what time he has left happy. In one way, it would be no hardship. I am of an age when most men think about settling down, having a family, and I certainly want children some day.'

'But...' Isabelle supplied when he paused, uncharacteristically hunting for words.

Because there had to be a but. It was there in his sudden hesitation, in the clouding of those brilliant eyes, the way his mouth clamped tight shut.

'No, don't bother, Luis—I'll say it for you, shall I? It would have been no hardship but for the fact that you are already married. To a thoroughly inconvenient sort of a wife. The sort of a wife that you thought you had got rid of, left behind you, years ago, and you never wanted to see again.'

She had never expected him to deny it, but, even so, his silence as she paused to draw breath had an effect like a blow to her face. He didn't even trouble to confirm her suspicions, simply stood there, regarding her stonily, no flicker of emotion on his dark features.

It was stupid, she knew, frankly naïve to have hoped for anything else. But she *had* hoped, she realised now. She had hoped that every word Catalina had said was a lie. That the inheritance of the dukedom had nothing to do with why Luis had wanted her back. And now she was being punished for that bit of presumptuous ingenuousness by the sharp slash of pain in her heart.

'So *why*, then? Why am I here?'

'You *know* why you're here.'

'No, I don't!'

She had thought she'd known. Had believed that even if he didn't love her the way that she loved him, then at least he had *wanted* her desperately—so much so that he couldn't live without her. But what Catalina had said had destroyed even that delusion.

'I mean, I know you needed a wife, but did it have to be me? Why not just get rid of the problem once and for all? I was asking for a divorce—why not just give me one? Why not divorce me and marry someone else—someone much more suitable?'

'Divorce wouldn't have been possible in this case, because our religion forbids it—certainly if I am to inherit my father's position. I cannot be divorced and also be Duque de Madrigalo.'

Isabelle almost doubled up under the impact of the brutal pain. The words were almost an exact echo of the sneering declaration that Catalina had made.

'Luis needs a wife. You're the only wife he has, and as his religion doesn't accept divorce—not if he is to inherit the dukedom—then you'll have to do. It's that simple.'

That simple and that appalling.

'And so you were forced to come to me? To ask me to come back to you.'

'I need you,' he had said. And he had sounded as if the words had had to be dragged out of him. As if he had hated speaking every single syllable.

'Isabella…'

'Are you going to tell me it had nothing to do with it? Because quite frankly I won't believe you. Your father made it plain that he believes marriage and the creation of heirs are your duty.'

'That's the way he sees it.'

'And you don't?'

He actually winced at the acid sarcasm in her tone.

'What do you expect me to say? That it never entered my head? We both know that would be a lie. But there was more to it than that.'

All he wanted to do was to take her in his arms and show her just how much more there had been to it. If he could just hold her, kiss away her anger and her fear, she might listen to him. Perhaps he could even tell her how close he was to proving it. But it was as if there were a glass wall between them, and her face had a frozen, hostile look that forced him to hold back. Her beautiful green eyes were just chips of emerald, icy and distant.

And the damn foolish vow he had made to himself also held him back.

'Of course there was *more*!'

From the black depths of her memories came the unwanted and unwelcome recollection of the night when they had made love. She could hear his voice, rich with dark satisfaction, when he had held her close.

'Now you know *exactly* why I want you back.'

Oh, yes, she knew all right.

She had let herself dream of a chance of starting again, of building a future together. But what would that future be based on?

Sex. That was all. She'd even been deceiving herself when she'd let herself call it *making love*. She knew different now. That deeply satisfied tone had told its own story. It had been rich with dark triumph, smug with the confidence of the conqueror. Luis had wanted her back to please his father, but once he had seen her he had wanted her for himself too. He had admitted as much. And she knew that what *he* wanted her for was *sex*.

He didn't want her as a wife, except in his bed. All he wanted was a warm, responsive body on which to satisfy his own desires, sate his lust. His heart was not involved in any part of this at all.

And she, poor, blind, besotted fool, had been every bit as responsive as he could have wished. She had given him exactly what he wanted. Exactly the sort of wife he had been looking for.

'Isabella…'

Luis was coming towards her. Hastily she backed away, holding up a hand to stop him.

'What does it matter *why* I wanted you back? You are back—and it's the future that matters from now on. The future we make together.'

He was going to kiss her; she could see it in his eyes. To take her in his arms and kiss all the anger, the defiance out of her. And if he did so then she would be lost. She would never be able to resist him.

'Don't touch me!'

Cold and hard, it stopped him dead, and she forced herself to meet the burn of his amber gaze.

'I don't want you near me. Is that understood?'

He didn't move a muscle. Perhaps something flickered in the depths of his eyes, but that was all.

'Perfectly.' It matched her tone, ice for ice.

'I don't want to talk about this—or anything—any more. I'm going to bed now—alone.'

If he had fought her, she didn't know what she would have done. But he made no move at all. Just stood and watched her as, with her blonde head held high, her back stiffly straight, she stalked past him and headed up the stairs.

She made it to her bedroom without breaking down. But when she sank down on her bed the tears would not hold back any longer. Too weak, too despairing to care, she gave into them and simply let them fall.

One large drop fell onto her hands as they lay on her lap and she wiped it away, her gaze going automatically to the beautiful ring that Luis had given her on her first night in the castle.

He might as well have stamped his brand on her skin, she thought bitterly, as burden her with this expensive proof of his possession. It was almost more than she could bear to think that the perfect diamond that gleamed so brilliantly might only be nothing more than a deception, a pretence, making a mockery of everything it stood for. Deep in her heart she knew that she would have welcomed something a quarter the size and a tenth as expensive if only it had come with the certainty of Luis's love she had once known.

But now it seemed that that love—and even the hope of it—was lost for ever.

CHAPTER SEVEN

ISABELLE stared at her reflection in the mirror and wondered just how she was going to get through tonight. Somehow she had to go downstairs to the main ballroom of the castle and greet the hundreds of guests who had gathered there, ready for tomorrow's ceremony. She would have to be polite and friendly, and make small talk, but most of all she would have to *smile*.

And smiling was the last thing she felt like doing.

It was impossible not to contrast the way she was feeling now with the excitement that had fizzed through every cell in her body on the night before what she now thought of as her 'real' wedding, two years before, in York. Then she hadn't been able to keep still, but had fidgeted from one task to another, too restless to settle to anything.

And as for smiling... Then her mouth had been stretched in one huge, permanent grin, and her eyes had sparkled in sheer joy and delight.

'Try!' she muttered now, directing the words furiously at her reflection. 'Try and smile! You look like you're going to a funeral, not a wedding party!'

But when she did try, then the exaggerated curve she forced onto her mouth looked like the painted-on grimace of a circus clown, totally unconvincing. And the green eyes that looked back at her were as dark and clouded as a mossy pool, no light showing in their depths.

'Wait for me in your room,' Luis had commanded in his phone call from who knew where earlier that day. 'I'll come and fetch you and we'll go downstairs together.'

A month ago, he had promised to be at her side throughout the ceremonies and the social events that would lead up to this wedding of theirs, and then she had been so happy, so thankful to think of his support that it had seemed, if not a sign of love, then at least an indication of some sort of caring enough to want to help her.

But in the days since then, everything seemed to have gone downhill so fast that it had made her head spin. After last night, Luis had withdrawn from her so completely that it was as if he had become a total stranger. And this afternoon he had simply disappeared, giving no reason for his absence, and he had delayed his return for so long that she had been forced to wonder if in fact he would be here tonight at all.

'Isabella!'

The knock at the door, the sound of her name startled her out of her miserable reverie. Of course it could only be one man. Biting her lip in an attempt to bring some colour into its bloodless shape, she hurried to answer his summons.

She was unprepared for the impact of his appearance. It had only been hours since she had seen him, but for some reason it was like seeing him for the first time in a long, long while. She had never before seen him in the formal elegance of evening dress, and the superb tailoring suited his tall form with stunning style. The cut of the jacket emphasised the width of his straight shoulders and broad chest. The trousers enhanced the narrow waist and hips, the long, long legs. And against the stark black and white, the deep bronze of his skin and the burning amber eyes stood out even more than ever.

'*Bueno*, I'm glad to see that you are ready,' Luis declared without any other form of greeting. 'And you look stunning in that dress.'

'*Gracias.*'

She resorted to one of the few words of Spanish she had learned in the hope of keeping her emotions under control. It was the first hint of approval she had heard in his voice for days and it brought hot tears springing into her eyes.

'I'm glad you like it.'

'I more than like it.'

The flare of desire in his eyes told its own story and one long, tanned hand lifted in an autocratic gesture, indicating that she should turn slowly in order to display the dress fully to him.

Her head came up as she obeyed him, a touch of pride coming into her own eyes. She knew that the deep rose-pink silk suited her, its rich colour warm against the creamy pallor of her skin. The fitted strapless bodice emphasised the narrowness of her ribcage and her waist, the swelling fullness of her breasts, and the long, flowing skirt enhanced her slender height.

'*Hermosa,*' Luis breathed when she finally came full circle to face him once again. 'You look lovely, but that dress needs a little something...'

From his jacket pocket he slid a slim, leather jewellery box and held it out.

'Wear this for me tonight.'

His tone startled her. When she had anticipated command, there was an unexpected softness in his voice and his golden eyes seemed to scorch her skin as he watched her take the box and flip it open.

'Luis...'

All words escaped her. Her eyes were blinded by the fierce glitter of diamonds, accentuated by the sudden burn of tears.

The necklace was a glorious river of jewels, delicate and spectacular, and the earrings that went with it were like the cascading tumble of a waterfall, curved and sparkling.

'They—they're perfect. But, really, I don't need...'

'Put them on,' Luis commanded huskily. 'I bought them with that dress in mind.'

He had known how they would look, he thought as he watched her move to the mirror, fix the earrings in place. He had imagined as soon as he saw them just how the diamonds would glow against the peach softness of her skin, the earrings falling in a scattering of stars from under the shining blonde hair and along the delicate lines of her neck. And the necklace just clasped the base of her throat, then spread out to fill the space above the line of her breasts, drawing attention to the soft beginning of the creamy curves.

'I can't...'

Isabelle was struggling with the fine clasp of the necklace.

'Here, let me.'

It was the first time he had touched her in days. The only time, in fact, since he had come to her room on the night of her arrival in Spain. And because of that Isabelle froze into total stillness at the first brush of his fingertips on her skin.

Everything that was female in her reacted to the tiny physical contact between them, sensation burning through every cell, spreading throughout her body like wildfire. With her head bent, the fall of her blonde hair coming forward to hide her face, she closed her eyes so as to concentrate better on the delicious feelings.

She hadn't realised how hungry she was for his touch until she felt it again and then her response was so instant, so fierce that she was sure he must feel it. That he must be able to sense the change in her breathing, the increased rate of her heart.

The fear of discovery made her flinch inwardly and immediately Luis froze behind her.

'Perdón—I'm sorry,' he muttered roughly, and as she glanced up swiftly her eyes met his in the glass of the mirror.

It was as if someone had tossed a bucket of icy water over a fizzing firework, dousing it immediately. His gaze was so distant, so withdrawn, totally opaque. With what physical closeness they'd had gone, there was nothing there but coldness and total lack of emotion.

It was the first time he had touched her in days. But not because he hadn't wanted to. Because he hadn't felt he had the right to act as her husband physically, until he did so mentally.

I didn't want forgiveness for something I didn't do! I wanted trust! The sort of trust that doesn't need proof—that believes in me completely and totally. Her words had hit him right where it hurt—in his heart.

Trust. He knew he hadn't given her that. He had walked out on their marriage in an agony of rage and hurt pride. He hadn't stopped to listen to see if there could be any other possible explanation, and he had stayed away, nurturing that anger all the time.

His fingers fumbled with the fastening of the necklace and Isabelle shivered slightly.

'*Perdón*,' he muttered again, automatically glancing into the mirror where he met the wide emerald gaze head-on.

'It doesn't matter.'

Her voice was soft and the look in her eyes made his heart clench sharply. How could he not have seen the truth in those eyes? The way that her soul seemed to shine out from them?

'It matters,' he said roughly. 'I want you to look perfect tonight.'

And then, because he had to hide his body's instinctive, automatic reaction to her, to the touch of the silken fall of her hair, the soft perfume of her skin, he swung away abruptly.

It was either that or take her in his arms and kiss her senseless. Kiss her until both of them were past thought and into the place where only the wild, urgent responses of their bodies mattered. And he'd promised himself that that would not happen—at least not until he'd made everything right. He'd been caught that way before, and he had told himself that it was what would get him through this. Now he saw that in fact it was what had been blurring his vision, blinding him to the truth.

'Luis?'

Isabelle's voice sounded softly from behind him. Clamping down hard on his baser instincts, he forced himself to turn slowly and face her.

In spite of the warmth of the evening, Isabelle felt chilled to the bone. His abrupt reaction had taken all hope with it. He was totally closed off from her. She couldn't even reach him physically. The distance he had put between them told her that.

And who had she to blame for that? Only herself.

Right now, she felt she would trade every bit of her pride for some of his passion if only it meant that he would look at her with *something* in his eyes. *Anything*.

'How do I look?'

Molten bronze eyes swept over her in a burning survey and her heart skipped a beat as she saw that she had touched him at last.

'You look wonderful.'

'Fit to be a duke's wife?' Her voice quavered on the question.

'You're fit to be anyone's wife,' he told her deeply. 'The question is more whether they are worthy of you.'

His tone worried her. She didn't understand the raw edge to his voice, the way a muscle jerked just above his jaw.

'What—?' she began but he held up a hand to silence her.

'No more questions, *querida*. Our guests will be here in half an hour, and before that I have one more thing for you.'

'Something else? Luis, I don't need another gift! I—'

'You need this. And it is not a gift. More like something I have owed you for a long time—far too long.'

'But...'

She frowned her confusion but he shook his dark head firmly.

'No more questions, come and see.'

He held out his hand to her and, unsure but trusting, she put her own into it and felt his fingers close about hers, warm and firm.

He led her out of the room, along the corridor and down the huge, curving flight of stone stairs to the main hall. As she moved beside him, each step in perfect harmony with the other, she couldn't help thinking that tomorrow she would walk with him in much the same way down the long central aisle in the cathedral.

She would be his bride, but not really his wife. She would have his position, his title, but she would not have what she most wanted—his heart.

'Luis,' she began uncertainly. 'You still haven't explained what will happen tomorrow—how things will go. We can't truly be married all over again because the ceremony's been performed. I know you said...'

'That you should leave that with me,' Luis filled in for her when she hesitated. 'And you have nothing to worry about.'

'But what are we going to do?'

'I have spoken to the archbishop and everything is in hand. Forget about it for tonight.'

Forget about it for tonight. The words echoed in his head, mocking him with their hollowness. How could he persuade her to do something that he found totally impossible himself?

Forget. He had thought of nothing else over the past few weeks. Thought only of how to make this marriage of his into a real one in every possible sense. And tonight was make or break time. With his free hand he touched his jacket pocket, heard the faint crackle of paper, and his heart missed a painful beat.

Tonight, he would put his fate in Isabelle's hands, and she would decide once and for all whether there would be any need to trouble the archbishop tomorrow or not. If things went the way he hoped, then tomorrow would be the start of a whole new life for both of them.

But if things didn't work out, then instead of being a beginning, tomorrow would be the exact opposite—an end to this marriage. Because if he couldn't convince her tonight, then he had no hope of ever enjoying a future.

He came to a halt outside the door to the library and forced himself to take hold of the handle and turn it.

'In here—there's someone who wants to meet you.'

'Someone?'

The expression on Luis's face told her that this was not just some new guest, some other member of his family she had yet to meet. His head was held high, his eyes meeting hers with an expression that she had never, ever seen in them before. Under the elegant jacket, his broad shoulders were taut with tension, and his breathing sounded strangely raw and uneven.

'Luis—what is it?'

He didn't answer. Instead he pushed open the door and stood back to let her precede him inside.

'See for yourself...' he said at last.

The woman in the library had her back to them. One arm resting on the ornately carved mantelpiece, she was looking up at a huge oil painting of a long-ago Duke of Madrigalo. But she was instantly familiar. Isabelle had seen that tall, voluptuous figure, the fall of long black hair down her back, only the day before.

Her breath escaped her in a jolting gasp and the room seemed to spin round her sickeningly.

'Catalina!' she managed through lips made dry with shock. 'What are you doing here?'

CHAPTER EIGHT

'WHAT are you doing here?' Isabelle repeated when Catalina didn't answer her, her black eyes going instead to the man still standing in the doorway.

'I...' she began, then obviously lost her nerve.

'Tell her!' Luis rapped out the command like a bullet from a gun.

'Yes—please,' Isabelle murmured. 'Tell me.'

What was Catalina doing here again? Why had Luis brought her? Because clearly Luis had brought her here. That much was obvious from the uncomfortable interplay between the two of them.

Turning to Luis, she was stunned to see he was actually backing out of the room.

'Why?' she began, but Luis shook his head, silencing her.

'This is between you and her. She knows why she's here.'

Isabelle could only watch in confusion as he left the library, shutting the door firmly behind him.

'Why are you here this time?' she tried again with Catalina.

'Are you telling me you don't know?'

Clearly the other woman had regained a little confidence with Luis's departure.

'I thought you'd sent that crazy husband of yours after me and told him to bring me here.'

'But Luis has never even mentioned your name. I never told him you were here.'

'But he already knew. He tracked me down where I was on holiday in America and said he wanted to see me. He even paid my fare back to Spain. That was why I was here yesterday.'

'You came to see *Luis*, not the duke?'

179

'I thought he wanted me back. So you can imagine how I felt when I found that *you* were here.'

The black eyes burned with jealous fury and suddenly Isabelle knew without being told that the story the other woman had told her the day before had been nothing but a lie.

'Luis found out you were here yesterday—and he wants you to tell me that everything you said then was just a pack of lies?' she hazarded nervously.

'That and the rest.' Catalina showed little sign of any repentance. 'He came to me today and told me that he only wanted me back here so I could apologise to you.'

'Apologise. For what?'

But deep down she knew and so, clearly, did Catalina. She looked most uncomfortable, pushing her hands deep into her jacket pockets, then taking them out again, shifting from one foot to another.

'For that night in York.'

And then of course there was no need to explain. They both knew exactly which night she meant. Just remembering, Isabelle shivered faintly.

'He sought you out so that you could prove to him that I was innocent that night?'

To her consternation, the Spanish woman shook her dark head emphatically.

'Now that I could understand. But, no—that's the weird thing. He didn't want me to *tell* him anything. There was no doubt in his mind that I was behind it all and that I owed you an apology.'

'You?'

Isabelle's head was spinning now. If Luis had brought Rob to her, to apologise, then that she could have coped with. But Catalina?

'Do you know how much I hated you?' The Spanish woman's tone was almost conversational but the way her black eyes flashed, the burn of anger in them, told its own story.

'Hated me?' She had never shown any sign of it. 'But I thought you and Luis had broken up long before.'

'Not long enough. I always thought we'd get back together. That one day we would be married. *Dios*, how I dreamed of being Duquesa! And you ruined all that! And I vowed I'd have my revenge.'

'You...'

Isabelle was remembering now. Recalling the way she had felt miserable, missing Luis and suffering with a cold.

'The tablets...'

'You thought they were cold relief, but in fact they were sleeping tablets. You were very young—a naïve, gullible fool. And Rob—ah, poor Rob! He was very, very drunk—and he had fancied you for months. It was the easiest thing in the world to persuade him that you had told me you fancied him too—to suggest that he might join you in your hotel room. After all, you had made it plain to anyone who would listen that you and Luis had rowed. All I had to do was to make him promise to lock the door...'

Her words rolled on, but they broke over Isabelle's head, not penetrating her thoughts. Instead, her mind was preoccupied with only one thing. A comment that Catalina had made earlier and that now was fretting at her brain, telling her something important.

'He didn't want any explanations,' she exclaimed suddenly, stopping Catalina dead. 'You said that Luis didn't want you to tell him anything. Just said he *knew*.'

'I assumed you had told him.'

Isabelle's head came up, a brilliant glow lighting in the emerald depths of her eyes. Her heart was singing, soaring in delight, and she couldn't stop smiling.

'No, I'd told him nothing. Nothing at all.'

Nothing at all. But he had believed in her enough to track down Catalina and bring her back.

He had *believed* in her!

Whirling round, she picked up her silk skirts and ran. Out of the library. Along the corridor, calling his name as she went.

'Luis! Luis! Where are you?'

Hot tears of joy were blurring her eyes so that she didn't

see him coming and ran head first into the hard strength of his body, reeling backwards awkwardly, almost falling to the ground. But powerful hands came out to support her, long fingers closed around her arms, holding her up.

'Isabella, *enamorada*, what has she done to you? I will kill—'

'No, Luis, no!'

When he would have moved away, furiously intent on finding Catalina, she caught at his arm and held him back.

'No, Luis.'

Half laughing, half sobbing, totally ecstatic, she caught her breath and looked deep into the blazing golden eyes.

'No, Luis, *enamorado*. There's no need for that.'

His own language got through to him where her English had not. She could feel the jolt of shock that ran through his powerful body, followed by an instant second of relaxation. But then almost immediately he tensed again.

'What did you say?'

Laughter bubbled up into her throat at the sight of his wonderful face looking so stunned, the dazed look in his eyes.

'I said, "Luis, *enamorado*,"' she repeated. 'What do you think I said?'

'But—do you know what that means?'

'Of course I know what it means! My Spanish isn't that bad! But if you'd prefer it in English, so that you know I know what I'm talking about, and that I mean what I say...'

She laid a gentle hand against the lean plane of his cheek, looked deep into the burning pools of his eyes.

'Luis, my beloved, my dearest, my darling husband. I love you and—'

But the rest of her sentence was stopped in its tracks, kissed away by the passionate assault of Luis's mouth, the pressure of his lips on hers. It was a kiss that scorched through every cell in her body, searing along every nerve, snatching the soul from her body and taking it captive for ever. It drove all thought, all hesitation from her mind so that she kissed him back willingly and happily and gave herself up to the force of his caress, her slender arms up around his broad shoulders, clinging on for much-needed support.

'I love you!' Luis gasped when at last he lifted his head to draw air into his raw lungs. 'I love you—I adore you.'

He punctuated each phrase with another kiss, drugging, mind-numbing, setting her head spinning all over again.

'You are my life, my whole reason for being. I can't believe how totally crazy I was to come so close to losing you.'

He shook his dark head in bitter despair at his own actions.

'I should have believed you, *mi angel*. Should have known that you could never betray me like that. I've been such a fool. Such a blind, stupid fool.'

'But even I never suspected Catalina,' Isabelle reassured him. 'I was blind there too. And you saw the light in the end. You trusted me, valued me enough to find her.'

'I would have walked barefoot to the end of the earth if it had meant that I could win you back,' Luis vowed and the depth of his words, the intensity of his voice, left her in no doubt about the truth. 'I couldn't have gone on without you. My life would have been empty—nothing.'

Another kiss enchanted her, made her melt against him, her blonde head going back, emerald eyes locking with bronze, oblivious of everything else. It was a long, long time before either of them could speak, but then at last Luis sighed deeply and, fastening one arm around her slim waist, he fitted her tight against him.

'I have a confession to make,' he told her softly.

'A confession?' Isabelle's momentary apprehension faded in the moment that she saw the warmth in his eyes, the glow that lit them from within.

'I would have come to find you anyway,' he told her huskily. 'I already knew that I couldn't stay away any longer. And when I got your letter it gave me just the push I needed. The fear that you might actually want a divorce—that I might lose you—was more than I could bear.'

He was pushing his hand into his pocket as he spoke, pulling out a large white envelope.

'This is for you,' he said gruffly, holding it out to her.

The look deep in his eyes told her how important the contents of that envelope were and her hands shook as she opened it, pulled out the papers it held.

'Luis—what? Divorce papers! But why?'

'If you hadn't believed Catalina when she told you what she'd done. If you'd still thought that the only reason I wanted you back was so that I could one day be the Duke of Madrigalo…then I would never have held you to our marriage. I had the papers drawn up ready just in case they were needed.'

'But that would have meant you… Oh, Luis!'

A choking sob caught in her throat at the thought of the sacrifice he had been prepared to make.

'You would have given up your claim to the title—and all that it entails—for me?'

'The dukedom and all its money, all the privilege, would be nothing without you in my life. Even if my position hadn't meant that I couldn't divorce, I would never even have thought of finding another wife. There could only ever be one woman for me and that is you…'

Once more his mouth took hers, making her moan softly with delight.

'My love for you is a once-in-a-lifetime commitment. I could never, ever marry anyone else.'

'And neither could I,' Isabelle assured him. 'You're the man I gave my heart to the moment I met you—the only man I'll ever love this way.'

But then a thought struck her and she caught hold of his hand, looking up into his handsome face in some concern.

'Luis—the wedding—what are we going to do? What are we going to tell everyone?'

Luis didn't hesitate even for the space of a heartbeat. This was what he had hoped for, what he had prayed might happen if he found Catalina and brought her here to tell the truth. It might prove a little awkward having to explain to his parents and their hundreds of guests, but, with Isabelle at his side, he knew that nothing else would matter.

'We tell them the truth, *querida*. Nothing else will do.'

Lacing her fingers through his, he gave her hand a quick, warm squeeze and led her down the corridor, across the hall. Pausing outside the door of the huge ballroom, he looked down into her wide green eyes, smiling reassurance into her concerned face.

'Ready?' he asked softly. 'We'll do this as we'll do everything else in our lives from now on—we'll do it together.'

And that 'together' lifted her heart, sending a rush of confidence and courage through her. It straightened her back, brought her head up high, put a light into her already brilliant eyes.

'I'm ready,' she assured him. 'With you at my side—as my husband—how can I ever be anything else?'

As the door of Luis's suite finally closed behind them, Isabelle gave a deep, heartfelt sigh.

It had been a long day. A long, perfect day. The sun had shone from dawn to dusk and there hadn't been a single cloud in the sky. In fact, there hadn't been a single thing to mar the day in the slightest way.

Of course, Luis's announcement that they were already married had caused some shock and consternation, but, once the surprise had died down, no one had truly minded. Instead, every one of their guests had been only too happy to attend the ceremony in the cathedral—only now the ceremony was to mark not their wedding but the renewal of their vows and to have their marriage blessed by the archbishop.

'Tired?' Luis questioned softly, hearing her sigh.

'A little.' Isabelle nodded. 'It is very late.'

In Spanish style, the ceremony hadn't started until seven in the evening and there had been a huge party to which all the village had been invited.

'I've danced my feet off.' She laughed, reaching up to unpin the beautiful lace mantilla she had worn instead of a traditional veil and then rubbing her temples wearily. 'And my ears are still ringing from all the fireworks.'

The first firecrackers had been set off as they had emerged from the cathedral and the explosions had continued all through the night, only dying away, reluctantly, as the faint pink threads of dawn had begun to creep through the night sky.

'It was a wonderful day!'

Through slightly misty eyes she looked down at her hand, softly touching the ring that gleamed there. A new ring for a new beginning.

It was of an unusual design, two hands holding a heart between them. And inside the ring was engraved the words, *'No tengo nada, porque darte.'* The design was taken, Luis had told her, from a ring that had been found in a sunken Spanish galleon. And the words meant, 'I have nothing, for it is given unto you.'

'The best day of my life.'

'The best?'

Luis had come behind her, strong fingers stroking the exposed nape of her neck, massaging weary muscles.

'Better even than our first wedding?'

Emerald eyes meeting bronze in the mirror, Isabelle considered thoughtfully, then slowly she nodded.

'Our secret wedding was wonderful—magic—but I was so young then. Little more than a child. I loved you but I was immature and unrealistic, I was just a girl; I didn't really know what I was doing.'

'And now?'

The way that the massaging fingers stilled on the back of her neck told her without words just how important this was to him.

'Now, I know exactly who I am—what I want.'

His slow smile was her reward, and the glow in his eyes intensified a thousandfold.

'And that is?'

In a rustle of fine silk, Isabelle got to her feet and laced her arms around his neck, pressing her lips to his in a deeply loving kiss.

'Now I'm a fully grown woman, my darling, with all of a woman's love for my man.'

'Is that a fact? So tell me...'

Once more those tanned fingers were busy behind her back, but this time they were unfastening swiftly and efficiently the silky ribbons that laced up the bodice of her dress.

'How do you feel about showing me exactly what this grown woman's love involves?'

Isabelle's smile grew, became wider, positively beatific.

'I thought you'd never ask. I can't imagine anything I'd like more.'

'A Dios gracias,' Luis muttered fervently. 'Because if I don't make love to you right now I swear I will—'

'You won't have to,' Isabelle interrupted, pushing her fingers into the black silk of his hair and drawing his mouth down to hers for a long, deep, passionate kiss. 'Because I feel exactly the same way.'

And as Luis swept her up into his arms and carried her towards the bed she smiled again in anticipation of the perfect end to a perfect day. It had been a day of public ceremony and public celebration but now, at last, this private time was theirs.

The world's bestselling romance series.

HARLEQUIN®
Presents

Seduction and Passion Guaranteed!

**Harlequin Presents®
invites you to escape into
the exclusive world of royalty
with our royally themed books**

By Royal Command

Look out for:
The Prince's Pleasure
by **Robyn Donald**, #2274
On sale September 2002

**Pick up a Harlequin Presents® novel
and you will enter a world of
spine-tingling passion and
provocative, tantalizing romance!**

Available wherever Harlequin books are sold.

HARLEQUIN®
Makes any time special ®

The world's bestselling romance series.

HARLEQUIN®
Presents

Seduction and Passion Guaranteed!

A new trilogy by **Carole Mortimer**

BACHELOR COUSINS

Three cousins of Scottish descent—they're male, millionaires and marriageable!

Meet Logan, Fergus and Brice, three tall, dark, handsome
men-about-town. They've made their millions in London,
but their hearts belong to the heather-clad hills
of their grandfather's Scottish estate.

Logan, Fergus and Brice are about to give up their keenly
fought-for bachelor status for three wonderful women.
Laugh, cry and read all about their trials and
tribulations in their pursuit of love.

Look out for:
To Marry McCloud
On sale August, #2267

Coming next month:
To Marry McAllister
On sale September, #2273

**Pick up a Harlequin Presents novel and you
will enter a world of spine-tingling passion
and provocative, tantalizing romance!**

HARLEQUIN®
Makes any time special ®

*Available wherever
Harlequin books
are sold.*

Coming Next Month

HARLEQUIN *Presents*

THE BEST HAS JUST GOTTEN BETTER!

#2271 AN ARABIAN MARRIAGE Lynne Graham
The first book in Lynne's Sister Brides trilogy, this story is
dramatic, passionate and deeply emotional—it has it all! When
Crown Prince Jaspar al-Husayn bursts into her life, Freddy realizes he
has come to take their nephew away. Refusing to part with the child
she loves, she proposes marriage to Jaspar!

#2272 ETHAN'S TEMPTRESS BRIDE Michelle Reid
The second Hot-Blooded Husbands book is a unique and
compelling story with vibrant characterization and hot, hot
sensuality! Millionaire businessman Ethan Hayes told himself that Eve
was a spoiled little rich girl, intent on bringing men to their knees. But
it was all he could do to resist the temptation....

#2273 TO MARRY McALLISTER Carole Mortimer
Read the final title in the Bachelor Cousins trilogy and witness
the Scottish hero trading his independence for romance!
Dangerously attractive Brice McAllister has been commissioned to
paint a portrait of supermodel Sabina Smith. Aware of their mutual
attraction, he moves the sitting to a romantic, remote castle in Scotland....

#2274 THE PRINCE'S PLEASURE Robyn Donald
Part of the miniseries By Royal Command, this book celebrates
our year of royalty with an exclusive wedding! Prince Luka of
Dacia trusts nothing and no one—least of all his unexpected desire for
Alexa. Torn between passion and privacy, Luka commands that Alexa
stay safely behind closed doors entirely for his pleasure....

#2275 THE HIRED HUSBAND Kate Walker
An unusual, fascinating and very sexy marriage-of-convenience
story. You'll love the gorgeous hero!
Sienna Rushford desperately needs to claim her inheritance—
but her father's will states she must be happily married! So she hires
Kier Alexander as a temporary husband—but Kier has a proposition
of his own....

#2276 THE NIGHT OF THE WEDDING Kathryn Ross
Best friends become lovers, in this enjoyable read with a sexy
hero and sparky heroine! When Kate asked Nick to pretend to be
her escort at a wedding he reluctantly agreed. But to his surprise the
pretense came easily. And as night fell the mood deepened into
something neither he nor Kate had ever felt before....

HPCNM0802